GUNS, DRUGS, And MONSTERS

GUNS, DRUGS, And MONSTERS

Written by
Steve Niles

Illustrations by
Ashley Wood

IDW Publishing
San Diego
www.idwpublishing.com

Book design by Robbie Robbins
Edited by Kris Oprisko

Published by
Idea and Design Works, LLC
2645 Financial Court, Suite E
San Diego, CA 92117

www.idwpublishing.com

ISBN: 0-9719775-2-6

05 04 03 02   4 3 2 1

Manufactured in Canada

IDW PUBLISHING is:
Ted Adams, Publisher
Kris Oprisko, Editor-in-Chief
Robbie Robbins, Design Director
Alex Garner, Art Director
Cindy Chapman, Designer
Beau Smith, Sales & Marketing
Lorelei Bunjes, Website Coordinator

Dedications

To my mom, Sally, and
my sisters, Jackie and Donna
            -Steve

For my own li'l monsters,
Max and Dante.
              -Ashley

chapter

01

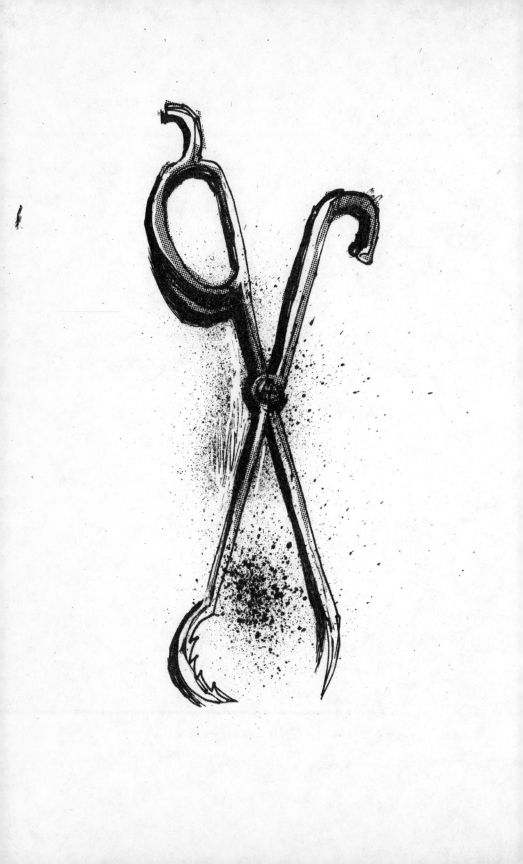

Something was going on that

last day of March, but I was too fucking out of it to realize. The city was getting on my ass. Everything about it—the people, the weather, even the monsters—was working over my nerves. I didn't know it, but I was itching for change. I was about to get a big dose of it, but I didn't know that either.

Twice, I noticed a black sedan outside my apartment. I figured it was the Feds looking in on me, as they would on occasion. But, this was post 9-11 and the Feds had better things to do with their time than put a tail on their favorite crackpot spook hunter.

In hindsight, I knew I was being followed. But that's what hindsight's all about, right? Trying not to look as retarded as you actually were by saying you knew something weird was going on?

The day started with my newspaper being stolen. In fact, all of the newspapers in my building had been taken. Then, while I was on the can spinning a three-coil monster of my own, the power went out. I had to finish my masterpiece, shower, and dress without light.

My head pounded. I was still more drunk than hung over. I'd lost a bundle to a bunch of ghouls down at the Black Cat Club. They always cleaned me out because I drank and they didn't. They'd bide their time until I was sloshed and then start hammering at me with outrageous bets they knew I couldn't turn down. Fuckers.

I decided to retrace my steps and head back to the Black Cat for a little breakfast drink. It was a crappy DC day. Rainy, soggy, and warm. Nothing kills a buzz as fast as a faceful of humidity. Outside was the black sedan, but I didn't pay any attention—even when it pulled away.

I got distracted by Brent, the postman/ghoul, on his daily rounds. He was a nice guy, well over a century old and as creepy as they come. He never crammed my mail into its narrow slot either. He'd always go the extra mile and climb the stairs to place it on my step.

"How's it going?"

Brent stopped and nodded as he shuffled bundles of mail. "Good, good," he said. "Looks like I don't have anything for you today."

"Probably just be bills anyway, right?" I gave him a little punch in the arm. In typical undead style he looked at his arm, then at me, before he smiled. "Yes, sure. I suppose so."

Most Ghouls have the sense of humor of a dead slug. They aren't big on jokes, kidding, irony, puns, or teasing. They did like riddles, but who likes riddles over the age of fucking five?

"You seen Mo'Lock?"

Brent shook his head. "Haven't seen him for a few days."

I looked around, giving the area the once over. "Neither have I. That freak-ass ghoul's always wandering off on me," I said, then looked at Brent. "No offense."

"None taken." He walked off to finish his rounds.

I shagged ass in the other direction and hiked the nine or ten blocks to the

Black Cat. The club looked like an old warehouse: a nondescript brick front with an unlit neon sign bearing its name. As I pulled open the door, I heard the blare of police cars in the distance, that sudden burst of noise that meant somebody, somewhere, was in trouble. I was just glad it wasn't me.

Inside, the club was dark. The bar was open, but the chairs were still up on the tables and the room smelled of dirty mop water. At the bar was Dante, a short, aging punk rocker with jet-black spiked hair. He was a fixture in DC; the kind of guy who would support the local music scene and run for city council at the same time. I liked to hang out in his place because I felt comfortable around the so-called "freaks". Everyone from Goths to Vegans hung out at the place. The last thing they cared about was some scarred-up old bastard knocking back shots at the end of the bar.

Dante looked up as I approached, but the usual friendly greeting didn't come. Instead, he just looked at me and gave me a somber nod. Something was bugging him. I assumed I'd done something the night before and had conveniently blacked out. I've been known to start a fight or two when I get loaded.

I slid up to the bar and tapped the rail for a beer and whiskey. Dante looked around and pulled a glass from beneath the bar pre-filled with frothy brew.

I tried to smile. "Expecting me, huh?"

Dante looked nervous, like he wanted to say something to me, but wouldn't. Or couldn't.

I sniffed the glass and swigged the whole thing down in one long gulp, killing my headache and bringing a warm calm over my body. By then, Dante had pushed a napkin in front of me with writing on it, but it was too late.

The napkin read, "DON'T DRINK THE BEER".

I looked at him. He stared. Suddenly, I knew I was in trouble. I could see Dante wanted to say something, but something was holding him back. I stood up and started to leave. As I grabbed for the door, whatever was in the beer began to crawl up the back of my brain and take effect. My head started spinning and my jaw went numb. I turned back towards the bar and saw a tall man step out from behind Dante, shoving him aside.

I stepped into the gloomy daylight as my arms started going numb and my eyes began to vibrate in their sockets like hot ball bearings. I stumbled forward, heading for home. One block. Two, three, four. Every step felt like I was dragging a wet sack of mud. I didn't have to look over my shoulder to know the tall man was behind me, patiently following me back to my apartment.

By the time I reached my place, I could hardly see at all. The world was a black tunnel closing in on me, and my unrelenting pursuer was right on my heels. I turned and got a good look at the man swimming in the murk. He was black, over six foot five, and wearing a tan suit with a tropical handkerchief in the pocket. I knew him, but couldn't place the name. I could barely place my own.

I stumbled up the stairs, fumbled with my keys, and crashed inside. When I spun to slam the door, the tall man was right there, smiling and backing me inside my apartment with a gun. I tried to stare at his face, but the muzzle of the gun was in the way. All I could see were his eyes, deep-set and bloodshot red.

The tall man kicked the door closed, smiled, and smacked me across the chops with the gun. I fell backwards and hit my head. Everything went black.

When I came to, I was tied to a chair. That I expected. What shocked me was that the chair was on top of my desk and the desk was pushed against the wall so that my back was against the office window! The shock of the revelation cleared my head like a cranial enema. I noticed the tall man standing nearby, waiting for me to eyeball him. Without the toxic muck on the brain I ID'd him on the spot.

His name was Dr. Polynice. He was a twisted fucker who chopped up kids, then reassembled the parts for reanimation. Once these zombie kids were brought back to life they were sold to sleazebag perverts all over the world. I put Polynice and his partners out of business a long time ago. He should have been rotting in jail.

"When did you get out?"

Polynice swayed on his feet. "Yesterday."

I nodded. "That would explain my missing paper."

"The escape made the front page. Guards died. It was very messy."

Polynice spoke with the slightest hint of a French accent. He'd grown up in Haiti, where he'd learned and mastered voodoo. Afterwards, medical schools in the States gave him the knowledge he needed to combine his arcane skills with modern medical science. He was one well-trained, learned, and sick motherfucker.

My gun was on the couch next to my knife, mace, and brass knuckles. He'd cleaned me out. Then I noticed the bag on the floor. It was a doctor's bag. One of those big black leather numbers, and I didn't have to see inside to know it was filled with all sorts of shiny, sharp nastiness. But Polynice opened it anyway, letting the light shimmer on the scalpels, surgical saws, knives, and syringes inside.

"You're not still pissed about that whole prison-for-life thing, are you?" I asked.

Polynice smiled pleasantly, saying nothing. He began to slowly retrieve one sharp instrument at a time, placing them on the desk in front of me like a waiter setting an elegant table setting. He set each instrument close, just out of my reach. It didn't matter. He had me tied so tight I could hardly breathe. All I could move were my toes, my head and the very tips of my fingers.

"You destroyed my life's work. You disgraced me, my family, and my profession," Polynice said in his island lilt.

"Profession?! Since when is being a psychotic pederast butcher a profession?!"

Dr. Polynice paused and looked me in the eyes. At his height, even though I was on top of the desk, we were practically at the same level.

"Do not confuse me with my clients."

By now he had six tools laid out. Any one of them could skin the flesh off my bones. "Oh, please! You killed those kids. You chopped them up and reassembled them, knowing full-well what some sick fuck intended to do with them!"

I saw the doctor shudder. He didn't like what I had to say. I saw an opening and jumped in.

"Come on, Doc, admit it. You were a little into it."

Polynice looked up from his instruments. "I brought dead tissue back to life. Mine was the power of the creator."

"But you killed 'em, Doc!" I laughed. "Come on, seriously, you made one of those little cuties for some personal fun time, didn't you?"

"I DID NOT!" Polynice slammed his fist on the desk, shaking. "I would... n... never do that to another..."

"Had a hard time in the clinker, Doc? Somebody bigger than you bend you over the bunk?"

Polynice looked at me. Tears were welling in his rabid eyes. His entire body was trembling.

"You put me there."

I glared back. "Fuck you. I'd do it again, and I will."

Polynice grabbed a scalpel and came at me. I'd already decided if I was going to die it wasn't going to be at the hands of this sick bastard. I pushed from the only place I had any leverage—my toes—and rocked backwards as hard as I could. As Polynice slashed at me, I fell back and went through the glass and out the apartment window.

I fell hard and fast, hitting the soggy pavement two stories below with a resounding crash and a shower of glass. The chair shattered, a couple of bones broke, and I lost some skin, but I was alive. I shook the ropes and shattered wood off and ran back in the building at full speed.

At the top of the stairs a panicked and horrified Dr. Polynice froze in his tracks. The look in his eyes was pure horror. Nothing like out-crazying the crazy. He didn't know what to do when he saw me with blood pouring down my face, flaps of skin hanging off my shoulder, and a big shit-eating grin plastered across my mug. He had three ways to go; up to the other floors, back into my apartment, or right at me. No matter what, he was mine.

Polynice chose "apartment," dashing suddenly out of my line of sight. I was on him in a split second and almost ran throat-first into his scalpel. Sliding underneath the doctor's clumsy attack, I rolled to my feet next to the couch where all my toys waited. I thought about grabbing the brass knuckles, but snapped up the gun instead. I had it on him before he could take a second slash.

Polynice dropped the scalpel and raised his hands. "You've got me. I surrender."

I shot him in the kneecap, and when he hit the floor I put another slug through his shoulder.

Dick.

0 2

The cops were pretty decent

about this arrest. They usually gave me a hard time, being an ex-cop and all, but the whole state had been looking for Polynice since he'd escaped. He had killed four guards and a nurse just to get his vengeance on me. What an idiot. For a doctor, someone who was supposed to save lives, Polynice had destroyed quite a few.

Plus, the bastard bled all over my apartment. There were holes in the hardwood floor from the shots I'd fired. The window was shattered. Rain was blowing in and the whole place had a thick layer of gunpowder and body odor floating right at nose level like milky fog.

Just then my landlord, Judy something-or-other, decided to stop by for an impromptu inspection of the building with some people who were along to assess for refinancing or some such shit. Judy was a dried up, little old lady—a strip of overcooked bacon in a jogging suit.

In the past, I'd managed to keep her at bay. I had "avoiding the landlord" and "pretending not to be home" down to an art. But when the cops dragged Polynice right by her, bleeding and squealing like a stuck pig, she would not be denied. The jig was up.

I smiled, but she didn't notice. She stepped through the open door and slowly scanned the blood, smoke and broken glass. Her face slowly turned red, starting at her shriveled neck and climbing right to the top of her small, bulb-shaped head like mercury up a thermometer. I dropped the smile. What was the use? She had me, dead to rights. It didn't help that I was three months behind on rent.

Even the cops still hanging out in the apartment sensed the tension. They packed up their shit and edged towards the door as the landlord slithered towards me.

"Strike three hundred, McDonald," she said. "I want you out of here by the end of the week."

"You can't do that."

"Try me."

She started counting on her fingers. "Unpaid rent. Running a business from your home without proper zoning or license, constant damage... and GUNFIRE!"

I glared down at her, but she stood firm.

"You're throwing me out?"

She nodded.

I spoke low. "I can get you the rent."

Now she smiled. A tight, wrinkled little smile. "You've been here for years and I've looked the other way. I'm tired of the noise. I'm tired of the police, the damage, the constant complaints. Did I mention the gunfire? I'm tired of having a non-paying tenant who gets shot at twice a week."

A couple of cops giggled like schoolgirls in the doorway until I leveled them with an evil glare.

I couldn't believe she would throw me out. I had zero in the bank. Make that zero with dust on it. I'd narrowly escaped being slashed to death by a Jamaican voodoo doctor. But this? This I found very upsetting.

I lowered my voice to a whisper. It was time to beg.

"I promise you, things will change."

"They certainly will." She wouldn't drop the smile. It remained plastered on her leathery face all the way out the door.

I just stood there, dumbfounded. The last two remaining cops were still in the hallway staring at me. I walked over and slammed the door in their smug faces. On the wall near the door, a *Speculator Magazine* clipping, brown and aged, hung from a tack. The headline read, "Cal McDonald, Monster Hunter". The picture of me was blurred and grainy. It was the only article Speculator had published about me that didn't attempt to make me out to be a total ass.

I ripped the clipping off the wall, balled it up, and threw it down. It rolled about a foot before it slowed and stuck in a small smear of blood.

I looked around the apartment, at the yellowed walls and scratched wood floors. I scanned the sunken brown couch with the exposed stuffing and springs. The only thing worth a dime in the whole place was my desk, my files, and the collection of weapons I had stashed under the bed in the other room. I bet if someone took the time they could find enough powder to get high for a year, but basically that was it. That was my life; some wood, some papers, and a sack full of sharp things.

03

While I stood staring at my

mess of a life, someone started tapping lightly on the door. It was an annoying little tap, but I knew who it was. I pulled open the door and Brent, the postman, stood there with a large square box. His face showed worry, but it always did.

"Guess I was wrong," he said. "You got this."

I took the box from him.

I stared at the short ghoul and turned my head. "Mind if I ask you a question?"

Brent sighed. "No, I suppose not."

"What did you do when you were, you know, alive?"

The ghoul looked puzzled by the question. "What do you mean, what did I do?"

"You know. What job? Were you an adventurer in the 1600's or some crap like that?"

"I was a postal worker."

He didn't even blink. If I'd offended him, he wasn't showing it. Then he timidly nodded and walked away. Fucking ghouls. They were harmless, loyal, and about as kind as a monster could be, but they were so fucking weird sometimes.

"Thanks, Brent!" I called after him and kicked the door closed before he responded.

Usually, nothing brightens the day like an unexpected package, but this one crawled up my ass and gave me the creeps right off the bat. It had an odd weight, heavy and shifting ever-so-slightly. It had a California postmark. The name and address on the label were mine, but there was no return address. It was trouble. I could feel it.

I used a penknife to slice the tape. The cardboard flaps popped open, eager to show me the gruesome sight inside.

It was a human head, severed clean just above the Adam's apple.

Weirder still, I knew whose head it was.

It was an old friend of mine, Sam "Hecky" Burnett. He was a private detective, and a hunter of the strange, bizarre, and outright freakish—just like me. The only difference between us was that he looked for the shit.

I've always tried to avoid the craziness and live a normal life, but not Sam. Not that insane old bastard. He savored the hunt. He loved tracking monsters like some folks love music or sports. He was obsessed, a fanatic. He had an encyclopedic knowledge of the supernatural, a mind like a thousand forbidden libraries, and I can say without reservation that he was one of the toughest son's-a-bitches I ever met.

Now he was just a head.

The look on his face was peaceful, like he'd fallen asleep and someone had made off with his body without waking him.

I hesitated, and then gave the forehead a poke. Nothing.

When I lifted the head from the box and moved it to my desk, the first thing I noticed was that the wound was almost completely bloodless. The slice was as clean as any I'd ever seen. In fact, the slice was so clean, it looked like it had been cut by a laser. It was so evenly severed, so straight, that I was able to stand the head on my desk by the stump of its neck without any other support.

Sam's head was covered with old scars from past battles. One ear was gone. The other was hardly a flap and a hole. His nose was bent and lumpy, and the rest of his face was a crisscross maze of healed hacks, scratches, and scrapes. Poor, ugly old bastard. What a way to go.

I sat in my chair and stared at the face of my probable future; the monster hunter, finally beaten. Finally outsmarted. Somebody, more likely something, had done this to him. Now it had been sent to me, I assumed, as some kind of twisted warning. Fuck them. It would take more then a head to frighten me. I wasn't scared in the least.

Not until the eyes fluttered. Not until the head moved.

I jumped back. Sam Burnett's severed head spoke.

"Cal?!"

The fucking head was alive! I jerked backward so hard that the legs of my chair dug grooves into the floor.

"Is that you, Cal?"

My chair tipped, toppled and I fell. I smacked my head against the hard plaster of the floor. I opted to stay there until it spoke again.

"Cal? Where'd you go, fer Christ's sake?!"

Slowly I peeked over the edge of the desk. Sure enough, Sam's head was sitting there, eyes wide open and alert.

I muttered, I stumbled, and finally spat out a somewhat coherent sentence.

"Hey, Sam. How you been?"

"I've been better, you big fuckin' pussy! Get off the floor and talk to me. We got troubles."

Despite the fact that I had a talking head on my desk, it was the "we" that bothered me the most. As I sat, I noticed Sam was smiling.

"You shoulda seen the look on your face. You were about as scared as I've ever seen anybody! Big bad detective, my ass! You're still a punk."

I felt my face flush. The head was right. I was lucky I hadn't pissed myself. "You wanna tell me what happened?" I said, hoping for a diversion from my embarrassment.

No such luck.

"Yer eyes popped out of yer head like two Ping-Pong balls," the head laughed. "What's the matter? Ain't you ever seen a decapitated head before?"

I glared at it. One more word and I was gonna punt him out the window. "You finished?"

"Haw!" Sam wanted to keep going. "Okay, Miss McDonald, I'm done. Big pussy."

I let the last jab slide. Despite the levity, something big and strange was up and I wanted to get to the bottom of it.

"Okay, fine," I said, "Now tell me what happened. Who did this to you?"

Sam's face went hard. "Damn kid."

"What?!"

"You heard me. I got bamboozled by a damn kid. An evil little son-of-a-bitch named Billy. Fifteen years old and smart enough to out-curse Aleister Crowley."

"A kid?!"

"Yeah."

"Fifteen?"

"You heard me, fuck-face."

Now, it was my turn to laugh, and I did. I let out a howl that made Sam more pissed than I'd ever seen him. But he was old enough and smart enough to know he had it coming. He just took it and waited for me to finish.

"So this kid," I said, "this Billy. What's his deal, and how the fuck did he do this to you?"

Sam rolled his eyes. "I was getting to that, so if yer ready to shut yer fuckin pie-hole, I'll continue."

Then Sam looked around the apartment as if he'd just noticed the glass and blood.

"What the fuck happened here?"

"Remember Dr. Polynice?"

"The guy with the thing for kids?"

"No. The one who helped that guy."

Sam thought about it a second. "The voodoo guy. I thought you put him away."

"I did... again."

Sam batted his eyes. I could tell he would have nodded if he had a neck—then went on. "Anyway..."

I took out my flask and swigged a hit as Sam talked. As I listened, I dug in my desk for any kind of pill. Anything to take the edge off.

He told me about a lead he had on some cult operating out of the Valley in Los Angeles. Some place called Sherman Oaks.

"You've been in LA?" I interrupted.

Sam looked annoyed. "Yeah. I like the heat, and work is pretty steady."

"So you got mailed from the other side of the country?"

"Yeah." He rolled his eyes

"How was the flight?"

Sam glared at me. "You want to hear this or you want to trade travel stories?"

I shrugged. No sense of humor. I found a yellowish capsule under some old cigarette packs in the side drawer. I wasn't sure what it was, but I hoped it was in the barbiturate family. This was no time for speeding.

The head noticed when I slipped the pill into my mouth. "I thought you quit doing all that shit!"

I swallowed. "The key word is all," I said. "I quit the hard stuff."

"Stuff'll kill you."

"I thought you had a story to tell."

Sam grunted and went on.

He told me about the Sherman Oaks cult. It was a devil cult with an odd calling card that caught the attention of local authorities. Evidently some pets—cats, dogs, a rabbit, and a ferret—had gone missing. One by one, the pets were discovered dead, flayed, and skinned like trout. Each pet was found at a different site in the woods surrounding the town, and at each site satanic symbols were found. Nothing too obscure or arcane, pretty much what you'd find on any respectable Metal album. Pentagrams and goatheads, that kind of shit.

The locals were freaked, but things got worse. Much worse. Kids started disappearing, babies and toddlers. That's when Sam was called in by a cop named Ted Dawson of the Sherman Oaks Sheriff's Department.

Sam got to checking around, and he found that it was more than just your run-of-the-mill, satanic-ritual-for-kicks case. There was some bad mojo going down. Strange things were suddenly happening around Sherman Oaks, California. Bad things. First, a teacher at the local middle school melted like butter in a microwave at a school assembly, and then some winged creatures were spotted plucking bodies from graves.

Sam was stumped until he tracked down a small crowd of teenage boys. All three—Carl Potter, Brian Hogue, and Billy Fuller—were your typical pimple-ravaged rejects. When Sam checked records at the local library, he discovered the three boys had checked out every single book on witchcraft and black magic, along with a half dozen volumes on alchemy and serial killers. Sam knew he had his suspects and he was ready to move in on them.

But something happened before Sam could lower the boom: Brian Hogue got hit by a hipster's pick-up truck outside a Bob's Big Boy in North Hollywood. The driver said the kid wandered into the road like a zombie and just stood there waiting to get hit. The truck dragged him face down on the pavement for half a block. He died on the scene.

Next, Carl met with a mysterious demise when he drank a gallon and a half of liquid drain cleaner as Sam walked up the steps to his house. Carl's parents said that they tried to pry the jug from their son's hands, but it was like he was possessed. By the time he'd emptied the jug, the drain cleaner had passed through the poor punk, turning his guts into liquid that poured onto the floor via his asshole. He died on the way to the hospital.

"So it was the kid Billy?" I asked, "He was the ring-leader. He was on to you and he killed the other two to sever his ties."

"Yeah, he was on to me, Einstein."

"How did he know *you* were onto *him?*"

Sam looked good and annoyed now. "I underestimated him. He heard I was asking around. I still thought I could walk up to the punk's house and haul his ass down to juvie."

But Billy was waiting for Sam when he arrived at the Fuller's ranch-style nightmare house. Sam walked right into a trap.

"When I looked down, I was standing in the middle of a magic circle he'd made out of the ground bones of the dead," Sam's head said, flushing with anger. "I was trapped, I couldn't move. Then the little brat shifted the dimensions between my head and my body. He separated me in two. Each part still alive without the other."

I shook my head.

"That is some fucked up shit," I laughed.

I knew the concept. Each second of time that passes is a separate moment in which everything exists. To put it in simple terms; if five seconds pass for a cow, then there are five different cows that can be tapped by dipping into the pool of time. What Billy had done was take Sam's head and place it in a slightly different time than his body, tearing them apart, but not killing them.

Smart kid. Evil as all hell, but smart.

"So, where's your body?" I asked.

"Somewhere in Southern California would be my guess."

I shook my head. "So how'd you... your head get all the way here?"

"The fucking punk dumped me off at Dawson's place. After old Teddy came to, I talked him into taking me to you."

I glanced at the box on the floor, at the postmark. Sam knew what I was going to ask before I asked it.

"Teddy chickened out. He mailed me."

I started laughing again.

"That's right, laugh it up!"

"I'm sorry," I choked, "I really am, but you gotta see the humor in it all."

Sam stared me down. "All I see is a bunch of dead kids and a crazed teen geek wielding power that can kill a bunch more. You gotta stop this Billy and get my fucking body back!"

Sam paused for a second, then screamed, "That's all I see... *you fuck!*"

He always made me feel all warm inside.

0 4

With all the over-the-top

shit I've seen in my day, I'm still not one for signs, but even I had to step back and look at this fucked up situation. I wake up, narrowly escape being killed, get evicted, and get a package with Sam's head and a desperate plea to go to California. The way I figured it, I'd been in the DC area my whole life. It was time for a change of scenery.

I decided to go to California without much hesitation. If you knew me at all, you'd know this was crazy. The closest thing to impulsive I ever did was snort two lines of speed instead of one. I generally liked the cozy insanity of the Nation's Capital, but lately I'd been feeling an itch for change. Things had grown stagnant lately. Same old cases, same old creeps, same old monsters.

Of course, I'd been off the hard stuff for almost a year. I suppose that had something to do with the itch. I'd go to California, stretch my legs, and see what there was to see.

But first I had some details to take care of, and my ghoul of a partner, Mo'Lock, was nowhere to be found. We had no formal agreement, but I'd come to rely on the fact that he'd pop by and help me out on cases on an almost daily basis. I'd known him for years, and undead or not, I considered him my friend. It wasn't like him to disappear for more than a week at a time. It had been *three* since I'd last seen him.

I made a few calls around town, with Sam grumbling at me from the desk the whole time.

"Screw your girlfriend," he snapped. "Let's get this show on the road!"

The head was right. I had more pressing business than finding Mo'Lock. I had to deal with packing up and blowing town. I also had to figure out how the hell I would get Sam's head back to California. I'd most likely be flying, and there was no way on God's Green Earth that I'd be able to smuggle a human head past baggage check. No way around it: I had to mail Sam's head back to his house and meet him on the other end.

"Like hell you are!"

Sam wasn't too pleased with the idea.

"You have any better ideas?"

Sam almost tipped himself over. "Yeah, we rent a private plane and…"

"You gonna pay for it? I've got a pocket full of lint and half a Vicodin to my name."

"So how you gonna pay for *your* plane ticket, smart-ass?"

Sam was starting to get on my nerves. "That's one reason I need to track down Mo'Lock. He can loan me the cash."

Sam rolled his eyes and grunted, "I shoulda called in some real law enforcement."

That did it. "You already did, and he mailed you to me."

I lifted Sam's head and dropped him back in his box. He yelled and even tried to bite me. I packed him in tightly, with packing paper in his eyes and mouth, then sealed up the box.

"See you in Los Angeles."

I resealed the package and scrawled "return to sender" across the label with a thick black marker, since Dawson had put Sam's home address as the shipper. Sam kept yelling and whining like a sixty-year old baby, so I gave the box a couple good hard shakes, then set it down while I surveyed my apartment.

My initial assessment stood firm; I didn't own shit. I packed some clothes, some books, and some papers. That was it. I made out a couple of labels with Sam's address on them and taped one to the box of weapons and the others to boxes full of shit I couldn't carry. If I had the time and money, I'd send for them. If not, I supposed I could live without most of it.

Mostly, I wished I could take the books. I had three shelves lined with volumes about everything from vampires to political conspiracy. They were the only thing besides drugs and alcohol I paid for.

Who knew, maybe I'd make it back before leatherface Judy threw it all out onto the street. I doubted it, though.

In only a matter of hours everything had changed. I looked around the office and thought about all the shit that had crawled through it and all the things that I'd fought and overcome. All of it started at that old desk. I ran my hand along the uneven surface and remembered the day Mo'Lock and I had stolen it from the office of a lawyer who represented a local fraud psychic who was selling curse cures.

His name was Doug Fleck—a big, fat, lying piece of shit. He actually had the balls to come around and look for the desk. I beat him half to death with a table leg.

Good times.

I got a little lump in the throat.

It was time to move on. I grabbed the bag I'd packed and kicked the package with Sam's head into the hall. I took one last look around. I'd miss it, but I knew I could do better. I flicked the lights off, and turned to go. That was the last time I saw my office-slash-apartment in Washington, DC.

0 5

It didn't take
me long to track

down Brent for the third time in a day. He was at the end of his rounds, which put him only a few blocks away. His truck was parked beneath a tree to block the drizzle as he sorted outgoing mail into small bins. He knew why I was there.

"I still haven't seen Mo'Lock."

"I want to send this back." I handed him the resealed package with Sam's head.

"You don't want it?" Brent looked side to side, then leaned in close. "There's a fella's head inside, ya know."

I nodded and smiled. "I know. I just need it to go back. I'm going to fly out and meet it on the other side."

I watched the ghoul's face as he worked out what I said. Suddenly, there was clarity. His eyes widened, his head bobbed, he gave me a wink.

"I'll make sure it gets back for you, Cal," he said. "Don't you worry."

A Yellow Taxi pulled up and the driver, another neighborhood ghoul, leaned out the window and softly honked the horn.

Brent and I spoke in unison. "Hey, Simon."

"You seen Mo'Lock?" I asked.

The cab driver shook his head. "Not since last week. You got something you need done?"

I rocked on my feet. I thought I'd sneak away clean.

"Well," I said, "it look's like I'm leaving town."

Brent looked shocked. "For how long?!"

"For good, maybe. It's time for a change."

"Is it us?" Brent asked sincerely.

I shook my head, "Of course not. It's just... I dunno. It just feels like the right time to make a move."

Simon and Brent exchanged a look of disbelief. They were shocked, but they thought I might be fucking with them.

Simon got out of his taxi and joined Brent and me at the curb behind the open mail truck. "You're joking."

"No," I shook my head, "I'm not. I have some business in Los Angeles, so I thought I'd scope the city out while I was there."

"Los Angeles, huh?" Simon rolled his grayish tongue in his mouth. "Bunch of freaks out there from what I hear. And I mean that in the worst possible way."

"And it's sunny all the time," Brent added.

I held my hand out and caught some drizzle in my palm. "It's gotta be better then this."

Simon extended his hand.

"You'll be missed, Cal McDonald. The city won't be the same without you."

Brent got a little choked up when he shook my hand. I gave him a slap on the back and he pushed me away. Funny little guy.

There was a long silence. Then Simon said what we were all thinking.

"What about Mo'Lock?"

I shrugged. "He's MIA. I gotta go. It's urgent." I nodded at the taxi. "You wanna give me a lift to the airport?"

Simon took my bag without saying a word and loaded it into the trunk. I said goodbye to Brent and asked him to tell Mo'Lock I'd left. Brent promised to spread the word around the ghoul populace that I'd be out of town for awhile. I didn't want some freaks crawling into town thinking the place was unprotected.

Simon drove me to the airport. He took the scenic route, twisting up and down every fucking street in the city. On the way we went past the police precinct where I'd worked briefly as a cop. I got thrown out, but that's another story. Suffice to say the massive intake of drugs and police work don't always mix.

It occurred to me that I'd forgotten to tell my old pal Blout I was leaving, but I hadn't heard a word from him since the Edgar Cain case. I figured he need to distance himself from me for the sake of his job. He was up for Captain. He didn't need me fucking things up for him. Another normy out of my life. And people wonder why I surround myself with freaks?

The farewell tour continued, passing the Black Cat Club, the scene of many a drunken brawl, and around Dupont Circle. Dupont was known for its gay community, but it also had considerable vampire traffic. I'd nailed a few blood-suckers to the walls of the tunnels beneath the Circle over the years.

Simon wove through downtown and down by the Mall where I got a final glimpse at the Capitol Building, the Smithsonian, and the Washington Monument in the distance. It was a funny thing. I'd lived in DC my entire life, and I never once went up in that fucking thing. I'd shot a creature who called himself the Master Eye off the top with a rifle once, though. He fell and exploded like a massive water-balloon.

As we moved away from the Mall, I spotted the Lincoln Memorial beyond the reflecting pool and smiled. Far beneath the memorial is a cavernous pit where the city's ghouls gather. To this day, I think I'm the only human that was ever invited to attend.

I caught Simon glancing at me in the mirror and dropped the stupid grin. I figured it was as good as any time to ask him what I needed to ask.

"You got any cash I can borrow?"

Simon's sunken eyes flashed in the rearview. "How much you need?"

"What's a plane ticket to LA cost?" I said. Most ghouls worked almost around the clock, but they didn't have much use for the cash they made.

"Yeah," he said after a short pause, "no problem."

The rain had slowed to an

annoying hot mist by the time the taxi dropped me off at the airport. It was crowded. A swell of people clogged the doors and the walkways trying to stay dry. I thanked Simon and walked away without ceremony. He watched me until a cop tapped his hood and told him to move it along.

Inside I bought my ticket and waited to board the plane.

For the first time, my thoughts went to what lay ahead of me. In DC, I'd come to understand the workings of the strange world in which I lived. Don't get me wrong, there were always surprises. Outbreaks of the undead or new forms of blood-thirsty creatures wandered into my path, but they knew I knew my way around, and that's what made me strong. Heading out to the other coast meant a whole new set of rules. God knew what the fuck lurked out there.

I've always attracted the darker side of life. Ghouls, ghosts, zombies, werewolves, mummies, vampires, and all sorts of nasty, unnatural creatures. I have two rules that I live by. The first is that I don't go after them if they don't come after *me*. Number two is to break the first rule if someone's got enough cash to make it worthwhile.

And this thing with Sam? That had me worried. What kind of kid could conjure up that kind of power? We're talking about something Aleister Crowley tried to do and failed. Splitting a human body into two different times was no easy feat. I'd seen it done before, but none of the victims had ever survived. Sam probably knew that too. The old bastard must've been scared shitless.

I thought about Sam as we boarded. There was the distinct possibility that I would never find his body and reunite it with his head. Who knew what the kid had planned, or what would happen to Sam's head if the body was hurt or destroyed?

The whole thing freaked me out, and I knew why. It was purely selfish.

Sam was me. He was an older version of myself, a glimpse into my future. Was this how I'd wind up? Slowly being whittled down to a scar-covered nub until I was eventually outmaneuvered by some psychotic freak? Fuck. I wanted to think I was more than that. I wanted to believe that I'd eventually move away from this monster hunting crap and do something else. But I'd thought about it for years—shit, my whole life—and it never happened. Every time I attempted to turn my back on the strange, it came looking for me.

As the plane took off smoothly, I watched my lifelong home fade below me through the small, circular window until it disappeared behind the clouds. Just like that, I was gone. I settled into my seat and stared out the window steadily for the next few hours. Mostly I saw clouds, but occasionally we dropped altitude enough for me to get a glimpse of the ground below.

As we passed over Kansas or one of those little farmy states I spotted a small object moving in and out of the clouds beside the plane. Whatever it was, it was small and fast as all hell. It easily kept pace with us, swooping in and out, up and down, as if fighting the tremendous air disturbance the wake of the plane caused. Finally it swung close to the wing and I got a good look at the object. It wasn't an object at all. It was humanoid, a small, naked creature with a rough tan hide and leathery wings that moved like a hummingbird.

I'd never seen one up close and personal, but I was pretty sure it was a gremlin, the annoying troublemakers of the monster world. And, just my luck, I had one tracking my plane. I looked around the cabin and, by the calm demeanor of the passengers, I guessed I was the only one who saw the creature. I determined there was a specific pattern to the gremlin's swooping flight pattern. It was staying out of sight, but at the same time, slowly moving closer and closer to the wing.

We've all heard the stories. The little creatures are reported to feed on metal and are attracted to the huge man-made flying machines. Gremlins became famous in the 1940's during the war as a friendly symbol of Air Force sabotage.

But behind every legend there's a little shred of truth, and this little bastard was intent on destroying the wing of a plane with over two hundred people inside. I had to do something without upsetting the passengers. Screaming "there's a man on the wing!" these days could land you in federal prison for twenty years.

The creature had been gliding closer and closer, and finally it started taking quick swipes at the underside of the far tip of the right wing. The sharp talons on its large webbed hands tore the metal like paper with each swipe.

I looked over and saw an old woman sitting across the aisle from me. I had two businessmen types in the seats next to me, but they were fast asleep against one another thanks to multiple rounds of Bloody Marys.

"Excuse me, old lady?" I said.

She looked at me with pure disgust.

"Do you have a hand mirror? I have something in my eye."

She looked at me for a long time. I blinked my right eye repeatedly for sympathy. Finally she dug inside her enormously overstuffed purse and took out a small round mirror smeared with lipstick and chocolate and handed it to me across the two sleeping suits.

"Keep it." She said and crammed her purse under her seat.

I felt like telling her I was trying to save her cranky-ass life, but what was the use? She'd just think I was nuts and demand the mirror back. Old bitch.

When I looked back out the window, not more than sixty seconds since I last looked, the gremlin was latched on to the wing like a starving leech. It was gnawing at the tip with long, sharp needle-teeth. Now that it was stationary, I could see it was no bigger than a medium-sized dog. Its body was shaped like a small, naked man with dried leather wings. The wings reminded me of thin slices of beef jerky.

The little fucker was going to town, chewing and biting and tearing. Each swipe of his talons brought sparks, shredded steel, and sometimes wires.

I took the hand mirror and aimed it out the window towards the wing. The sun was behind the creature, so I tilted my hand up until the mirror caught the light. I reflected the beam back down towards the thing on the wing. The air was a little rough, so I had a hard time catching the little fucker with the beam, but I finally managed to level it right at his face. At first, it just lit up the gremlin's wide, ugly face. Fucker didn't even seem to notice until I shined the light into its eyes.

The gremlin looked up in a shot and squinted. Its eyes were perfectly round saucers of black, like headlights filled with darkness. I held the mirror as level as I could, keeping the beam aimed straight at its eyes. The stubby creature started to get agitated quickly and stopped gnawing on the wing. It swatted at the light with its claws, trying to knock it away. It got flustered and confused when I moved the light to its chest. It tried to brush it away and actually cut itself with its own claws.

It was a far better reaction then I'd anticipated, so I aimed the ray of light right at the gremlin's exposed genitals. The creature clung to the wing with one paw as it watched the light crawl down its body. When the beam stopped on its crotch, the creature swiped hard with its own talons and mutilated itself.

There was a stunned moment where the creature stared down at his shredded genitals with utter disbelief, then it lost its grip on the plane's wing and fluttered away like a trash bag in the breeze.

* * *

The flight was fairly uneventful after the gremlin incident. The suits next to me woke up over Arizona and started drinking again. The old woman read and reread the in-flight magazine so many times I wanted to slap it out of her hands, but that was about as exciting as it got.

As we descended into Los Angeles, I looked out the window and saw the desert and mountains turn to endless acres of homes with tiny, bright blue circles beside them. For a moment, I couldn't figure out what the circles were. Then I realized they were backyard swimming pools. I'd never seen so many pools in my entire life. They were everywhere.

That was the first tip that I was heading into some strange and unusual territory. Arriving at LAX was the second. The place was like nothing I'd ever seen and was crawling with ghouls, freaks and unnatural beings of every variety known to, well, me.

I made my way out of the gate and spotted a couple of ghouls working a shoe shine stand. I gave them a nod. They just stared blankly and turned away. Nearby, a group of what looked like Armenian undead looked me up and down as I passed. To tell the truth, I didn't know exactly what they were. I could see they were dead, but the sun was out, so they weren't vampires. One thing was for sure: they reeked of evil.

I kept moving through the airport and everywhere I looked something stranger waited. It wasn't always something unnatural, at least not in the classic sense. I saw women with their skin pulled so taut on their face that I could clearly see their skulls beneath the tight flesh and caked make-up. I saw men with suntans so deep that their flesh resembled old beef jerky. I witnessed some of the most bizarre fashion I'd ever seen, and I don't mean punk rock weird. *That* I like. I mean huge gold sunglasses and white bellbottoms with feathers and rhinestones on a sixty pound woman who looked like she hadn't eaten since 1998.

Los Angeles would take some getting used to.

Everyone else veered towards baggage claim, but I'd reduced my life to one bag, so I made straight for the taxi stand downstairs. On the way, I had to walk through an army of pamphlet peddlers and beggars, all of them human. On my right a Scientologist flunky shoved a book at me. I slapped it away. On my left a Hari Krishna asked me how I was doing and tried to block my path. I plowed over him like a bulldozer.

Outside, the biggest shock of all waited. I stepped out of the air-conditioned building through the automatic doors and into the heat... and it was nice. It was hot, but the air was dry. It was nothing like back in DC where the humidity climbed to a suffocating ninety-eight percent. Of course, DC was built on top of a swamp. This was desert weather. I couldn't believe it. I stood outside in the bright sun and enjoyed it. Now *that* was strange.

0 7

The cab driver wasn't a ghoul.

He was an old black man who never so much as glanced at me through the rear-view mirror. I gave him the address for Sam's place and he took off like a bat out of hell. I expected to get a nice tour of the streets of Los Angeles, but instead the driver introduced me to the high-speed world of California freeways. I hadn't seen driving like that since I ran the speed course at the police academy. We were doing at least ninety-five and weaving in and out of lanes so fast I was thrown from one side of the back seat to the other like a rag doll.

About forty minutes and a hundred bruises later, the driver spun off the freeway and onto some actual city streets. It was here I caught the driver looking at me, and he spoke at last.

"First time in LA?"

I was crawling off the floor of the cab. "Yeah."

"Well, a fella that's never been to LA needs to see some sights," he said with a strange drawl. "How about I show you a movie star's house?"

I shrugged. "Sure. Sounds good." I was in no rush.

The driver careened wide around corners and over hills, until the scenery around us changed from distinctly urban to something like residential. The streets were unnaturally clean and the houses were huge, but what really struck me as odd were the palm trees lining the streets. You never saw anything like them back East, unless you went to Florida. But who the hell went to Florida?

He finally came to a stop at a corner where he pointed at a modest, but by no means small, Spanish-style house.

"See that?"

I nodded.

"That's the home of Mr. Don Rickles."

I stared. "Wow."

And that was the end of the celebrity homes tour.

The rest of the ride was a blur. The cab drove me down Sunset, which was all expensive shops and stores before turning into a solid mass of flashy signs and restaurants. From there he drove down an alley-like back road that wound like a snake, climbing steeply uphill before peaking and spilling us down on the other side. I knew enough about LA to realize we'd left the city proper and were headed into the dreaded San Fernando Valley.

The trees were more normal on this side of the hill, but the number of butt-ugly strip malls doubled, and the whole area was flat as a board. I could see hills through the haze in the distance, but it was mostly endless suburbs as far as the eye could see. Talk about fucking scary.

Almost as soon as we drove over the hill, the cab made a couple of quick turns into a strange little residential area with single-story, squat-looking homes that resembled adobe forts, except these little forts had bars on the windows and graffiti tags all over the walls. I couldn't make out any of the graffiti. To me, it just looked like a bunch of spray-painted circles and squiggles.

The street looked rough, a compact ghetto made just for me. Kids were standing on the sidewalks in clusters, watching closely as the cab pulled up. I could feel their eyes on me, checking me out. I saw one kid point and another whisper to his partner as he checked his waistband for his gat.

They looked like they were going to start something until the cab stopped in front of Sam's address. Then they all turned their backs.

I laughed. Sam must have scared the crap out of them.

I paid the driver and thanked him for the tour. He sped out of there without saying a word. I hoisted my bag and walked toward the door, ignoring the eyes that watched my every step.

The yard was fenced in by a low, rusted chain-link fence. There wasn't a lawn to speak of, just a lot of dirt that looked like it had been dug up recently. The dirt was unsettled all the way around both sides of the house, like someone had started planting some shit then gave up.

The rest of the house was no prize. The white stucco walls were yellowed and stained, the gutters were broken and the red clay shingles on the roof were cracked and split. The porch had once been a screened-in area, but someone had torn out the wire mesh and removed the door. Now all that remained was a green wooden frame around the outside of the deck. The place was a complete shit-hole.

At the door, I found the key Sam had hidden. Next to the mail slot was little piece of paper about the size of a fortune cookie strip that read "Burnett Investigations". Classy.

I unlocked the door and went inside.

It was pretty much what I expected, an old man's version of my place in DC. It was part home, part office. There was a desk and a couch, some file cabinets, all kinds of clippings and weird pictures taped and tacked indiscriminately all over the walls.

It was a lot messier then my place. Actually, it was fucking disgusting. There were old food containers on the floor with both large and small black pellets along the walls. It looked like a wide variety of rodents used the place as a toilet. I cleared the couch of crap and threw my bag down.

The front step and mail box held no delivery slip—there was nothing but a pile of junk mail. I'd beaten Sam's head across the country, and without the

head there wasn't a hell of a lot I could do, so I raided the liquor cabinet. It was
the one thing that looked to be well stocked. I helped myself to some whiskey
and beers and turned on the TV. Just when I had a decent buzz going, I heard
footsteps outside the door. I reached for my gun, and realized it wasn't there.
Then there was a knock.

0 8

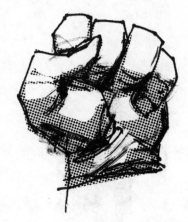

The knock sounded timid,but I wasn't

taking any chances. I found a Colt .45 in Sam's desk, checked to make sure it was loaded, and approached the door.

"Who's there?

From the other side of the door I heard, "Jerry."

"Who the fuck is Jerry?"

"You don't know me."

Fuck.

I tucked the gun away and yanked the door open. Jerry stood on the porch looking nervous. He was a kid, I'd say around eighteen or nineteen. He was shaking, with sweat running down his face. With some people you can see who they really are when they're afraid. This kid's eyes read innocent. I decided to give him a chance.

I gestured him inside, checked the street, and then shut the door.

The kid bobbled around the room before sitting on the couch. "I'm Jerry—Jerry Gallagher."

I gestured for him to go on. "And?"

"I've never done this. I'm not a narc or nothing, and I'm not even sure if anything is happening, Mr. Burnett."

I fought the urge to laugh. The kid thought I was Sam. He was here looking for help. I thought about saying something, but decided I was bored and went along with it. Shit, I had to wait for the head anyway. Might as well kill some time. What's the worst that could happen?

"Well, why don't you tell me what you think might be going on," I said, trying to guide him along.

The kid took a breath. "It's my roommates. I live in this loft downtown, you know, near Staples Center?"

I shook my head. What the hell was a staple center?

"Well, I've only been there a month or so, but I've been getting weird feelings about these two guys. There's five of us all together."

I nodded repeatedly, praying he'd get to the point. I found a pill in my pocket, probably speed. I hoped it would balance me out. The whiskey mixed with the time difference was making me woozy. My buzz was officially killed.

"Anyway, John and Sean live downstairs in the basement. At least that's what we call it, cuz it's below street level and doesn't have any windows. The rest of us live upstairs, and at first we thought maybe they were fags or something—which I wouldn't really care about. But now, I think something else is going on." The kid stopped and looked at me stupidly.

Suddenly I wanted to rip him off the couch and strangle him. He talked so much and so fast my head started to ache. But I egged him on anyway.

"And just what makes you think something else is going on between this Sean and John?"

Jerry sucked air to fuel up for his next rant. "Well, I hear noises down there late at night. Weird noises. At first I thought it was, you know, fag stuff. But then the other day they left the basement unlocked. They're usually real careful about keeping it locked. Anyway, I went down there with my other roommate, Myra—she's scared too—and we found this freezer. We opened it up and..."

The kid produced a small baggie, fogged with steam. "We found this inside. I kept it in the freezer upstairs 'til I decided to come here."

I took the baggie from Jerry and sat at Sam's desk. The bag was still cold. It was the "zip-lock" kind and it opened easily. The contents thumped onto the desktop—a human hand. A small, frozen, dismembered baby's hand, clenched in a tiny fist.

"Think you got something here," I said, poking the hand with my pen. "Are you the only one who saw this or who knows you have it?"

"No, Myra knows, but she's the one who talked me into coming to see you, Mr. Burnett."

I thought about coming clean with the kid, but blew it off. What did it matter to him what freak hunter he was dealing with?

I slid the frozen hand back into the baggie and looked over at the kid. I spoke nice and slow so I wouldn't slur and he'd understand the plan.

"I want you to take this back. Do you think you can get it back into the freezer without tipping off John and Sean?"

"I think so. Myra swiped a key off one of their desks. I don't think they noticed."

"Good, then put it back and announce that a friend from out of town is visiting. I'll be there around six."

Jerry looked me up and down. "You're kinda old."

I glared. "Then tell them I'm your retarded cousin from Alabama. I don't care, just make it sound good. I need to get in the house."

I escorted him out, getting the address and making doubly sure he understood the plan. I think he got it, but I was still nervous because he was. Nervous people screw up cases more than just about anything else.

He turned back to me. "Oh—uh—about money. How much is this going…"

"I knew the second you came in this was a freebie, kid. Pay me in beer," I shut the door in his face.

Back at Sam's desk I dialed info and got some numbers for local hospitals. I had them patch me through to the maternity ward. After four duds, I got some guy at a downtown hospital who could barely speak English.

"This is Dr. Jacobs, up in records," I said in a high whine. "Can you give me the numbers on the missing infants again? I can't find mine anywhere."

There was a pause, and I thought I was busted. "Ah, jes, jes, Doker. This the same as jesterday. Jus' two. One Tuesday, an' one Thursday."

Bingo.

I slammed the receiver down. The hand looked newborn. It was too small to be much more than a week old. So, it seemed I had kidnappers on my hands, maybe Satan worshippers, or even cannibals. That would explain the freezer. That, or they were keeping it frozen to dispose of later. Whatever it was, these were sick fucks, and I had me a new case to kill the time until Sam's head showed up in the mail.

chapter

0 9

First thing I learned about LA

is no car, no life. After Jerry left I had a few more drinks, then stood outside the house waiting for a taxi that never came. I stood there until it got dark. A small crowd of kids with bald heads and wife-beater tees were watching me from a house down the street. After I'd stood there for awhile, two of the teens strolled down and crossed the street to where I stood.

They were both Hispanic, and covered with tattoos. The older of the two had a teardrop tat beneath his left eye. They stood there staring at me for almost a minute before I turned and gave them a nod.

"You Sam's kid or something, dude?" Teardrop said.

"Just a friend."

"You waiting for something?" the other asked. "Looks like you're waiting for something."

"Trying to catch a cab."

The two guys busted up. They started laughing, falling all over each like I'd just told them the funniest damn joke they'd ever heard. I stuck my hands in my pockets and nodded while I waited for the comedy show to stop.

Teardrop slapped my shoulder. "Where you from?"

"DC," I said.

"Oh, well, out here they ain't got cabs that drive around 'less you in Hollywood or some shit like that. Here you have a car, or steal a car if you have to. I'm tellin' you right now, ain't no cab coming on this street."

I looked at Teardrop and his buddy. "Rough neighborhood?"

They started to laugh again. "Don't look at us, man! Cabs don't come down this street cuz of your buddy, Sam. Shit, ice cream trucks don't even come here no more. That's one fucked up dude you got for a friend. I mean, we're cool with his ass and all, but he sure does have some weird-ass shit comin' around."

"My name's Cal," I said and stuck out my hand.

We shook. Teardrop's hand was bone cold.

"Welcome to the neighborhood. You staying around awhile?"

I shrugged and stared into Teardrop's eyes. "Maybe."

Teardrop touched the Sacred Heart tattoo on his chest with one hand and gestured to his buddy with the other. "My name's Benito and this here is Junior."

Benito concluded with a wide smile and I saw the fangs. He meant for me to see them. The boys were vampires, but I'd seen them in the sunlight, so something wasn't right.

"Good to meet you."

We all stood there in silence for a while. We were all smiles, but we were checking each other out, trying to figure whether we had a problem. Usually when I stood this close to a vampire I was either killing them or thinking about killing them. These guys didn't give me the slightest bad vibe. I decided to open the dialogue.

"You know another thing that's different here from DC?" I said.

Junior responded. "No, what's that?"

"In DC, vampires can't walk around in the sun."

Benito looked at Junior and nodded, then they both looked at me.

"We ain't full-blown," Benito whispered. "That's why Sam don't stick a stake in our heart and shit. We can live off raw meat and, you know, the occasional snack."

"But we don't never hurt nobody, 'less they ask for it," Junior added.

I waited a few seconds then smiled.

"Then it looks like we're okay."

Benito gestured towards me. "So, you need wheels? You got some money?"

"A little."

"My cousin owns a rental place. You go there and he'll hook you up. Just tell him Benito Cruz sent you."

Benito called his cousin and told him to expect a big ugly white dude, then gave me walking directions to the lot. I thanked the semi-vampires and walked off. It was the first time in my life I'd turned my back on a vampire, but true to their word, they didn't attack. Nice neighborhood.

*　　●　　▸

Benito's cousin's lot was a little dump of a place off Ventura Boulevard, but he had a nice selection of cars. I laid down a decent chunk of the cash Simon had loaned me and got set up with a jet-black '63 Pontiac Catalina. The car roared like a fucking lion. I probably should have went with a cheap Honda Civic or something, but the Catalina just cried out to me. Besides, I'd look like a jack-ass in the Civic. I put down as much cash as I could, but because I was "friends" with Benito, the cousin would let me pay off the balance later.

I rumbled from Ventura to the freeway and headed towards downtown Los Angeles. It was way past the time I said I'd meet Jerry, but I figured he'd wait.

1 0

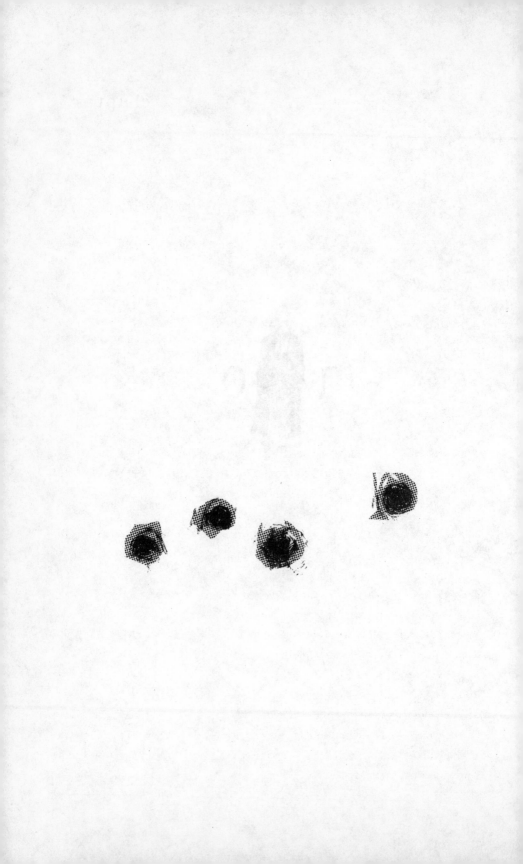

I arrived at the warehouse loft

a little before eight. The street was deserted. Strictly urban. I saw a couple crackheads milling around an alley, but that was it. I guessed down-town LA wasn't the happening spot for hipsters or the undead.

The pill I popped had hit a little harder then I'd expected, so I was pretty jumpy. I parked my new ride outside the drab building. It was flat gray with clouded, dirty windows and a door that looked like a loading dock. I hit the intercom beside the double steel doors.

No sooner had the bell rung than a voice started yelling from somewhere inside. It was a female voice, high pitched and panicked. She screamed that she'd be there in a second. My guess was that it was Myra.

Bingo. She answered the door wrapped in a towel, and her hair was dripping wet. She had a tattoo of flaming dice on her right shoulder and a tribal design around her wrist. Her hair was black and cut with shorter-than-Betty Page short bangs. I guess I was wrong about the hipsters.

"Oh, I thought it was Joey. Sorry, you must be Jerry's friend. Uh, you want to come in?"

"Yeah, that was the idea."

She pulled the door open a little more, told me to make myself at home then scrambled up a cold flight of cement stairs. As I entered the warehouse, I noticed the stairs didn't go down any further. If there was a way into the basement that Jerry mentioned, I couldn't see it.

I followed Myra up the stairs. She was small and thin and looked like a spider monkey as she took the steps two at a time. Her towel had come open in the back. I looked away.

At the top of the stairs a door led into the loft. It was a wide open space with all sorts of mismatched furniture scattered around. There was artwork plastered on the walls and even a motorcycle being worked on in the far corner. There were beer cans by the case stacked neatly in the corner near a hand-written recycling sign. The walls were covered with haphazardly hung concert posters by artists like Coop and Shag. It looked like Jerry and his pals were full-blown, creeper-wearing hipsters.

Above a sunken foam couch was a poster of John Travolta with his eyes gouged out, his teeth blackened and horns drawn onto his forehead. I threw my bag aside and sat on the couch. In an area I couldn't see, I could hear Myra running back and forth, muttering loudly to herself about her hair. I wandered around the loft and glanced out the windows at the back of the building. Instead of the expected alley there was a small yard with grass and a fenced-in garden. I had to give the kids credit, it was quite a swinging pad.

As I lit a cigarette and settled back, I began to wonder where my little pal Jerry was. He knew I was coming. The little prick had better not have flaked on me. I'd strangle him for sure.

From the couch, sagging to the point where I nearly sat on the floor, I could see the door to an old fashioned, steel-caged service elevator. That was your basement access right there.

After a couple of minutes, Myra appeared again. She was just sort of standing there, smiling, and staring at me as though she were sizing me up.

"You don't look like a detective," she said, walking toward me.

Fucking great. Jerry told her. Stupid kids can never keep their mouths shut.

"Well, that's the point of being undercover. Any idea where our boy Jerry is now?"

She sighed. "No, I haven't seen him since he got back from your office." Then she looked me over in an odd sort of way, with her head tilted to one side. "How old are you?"

"How old do I look?" I shot back.

"Anywhere from 25 to 45," she smiled. "I can't decide."

I felt myself begin to flush red. "Somewhere in the middle."

Myra smiled pleasantly and adjusted her bangs without ever once taking her dark, intense eyes off me. Just when I thought she'd embarrassed me enough, she took another step. "You seeing anybody?" she gestured at my ringless hand. "You're not married."

I stared at her blankly, stunned, like she'd just asked me where the sky was located. What a stupid question.

Despite thinking much more, all I said was, "No."

Myra looked puzzled. "Why'd you say it like that? When was the last time you dated someone?"

That tore it. I leaned forward. "Hey, who's doing the investigating here?"

But she was unshakable. "It's been a long time, hasn't it?"

I usually have two responses to being cornered. One leaves somebody bloody on the floor. The other results in a lot of running. Because Myra was so attractive and straightforward, I chose neither and just answered the question.

"I don't date," I said. "People I like tend to wind up hurt... or worse."

Myra looked at me for a long time, but she wasn't judging me. She was trying to figure me out. Then she stopped and glanced toward the door. She looked back at me and nodded. Somebody was coming up the stairs.

After a moment, two guys appeared at the top of the stairway. John and Sean, I guessed. One was tall, with red hair and an expression somewhere between grim and nasty. He wore a silk skull and crossbones shirt with jeans rolled in fifties cuffs. The other guy was a bit shorter, but pleasant looking, with blonde, slicked-back hair. They looked to be in their mid-twenties and both had big green army duffels slung over their shoulders.

Red walked right through the room without even so much as glancing our way and went straight to the service elevator. After noisily opening the cage, he waited impatiently as the blonde stopped in front of us and placed the duffle down on the floor. I could see by the way the muscles in his forearms strained and relaxed that the load wasn't light.

"Man, that laundromat is a fucking pain," he said, and extended his hand to me. "Hi, I'm John. You must be Jerry's friend?"

We shook hands as I nodded and fake smiled. I lit a cigarette and watched him as he leaned over and picked up the bag. His legs tightened. His calves flexed. That was some heavy laundry. After flashing another grin, he met Red (who I assumed was Sean) in the elevator.

Myra was staring at me. "You want to go get some beer?" she asked.

"Yeah," I said.

I needed to talk to her. I got a distinct freak vibe off of both John and Sean, and I'd seen bags with that kind of weight before. The bags were either filled with bricks wrapped in cloth or chopped up body parts, and the baby fist seemed to support the second possibility. Nothing weighs down like human tissue.

I didn't say anything to Myra, but I had the horrible feeling Jerry was in those duffels.

We left the loft and walked along the deserted streets. It was dark and about as empty as any urban downtown that I'd ever seen. Some cities are like that, even parts of DC. There are city blocks that are only populated during the work week. At night and on weekends, they become ghost towns.

"The walk was a good idea," I said as we strolled.

"It wasn't all a lie. We do need beer." Myra watched the ground as she walked, as though she were searching for something.

The speed had washed away the effects of the drinks I'd had earlier. I was getting shaky and it was getting difficult for me to sift through the facts in my head. I wanted another hit, or maybe something else to soothe me. It was strange; being in a new town had a sobering effect. It seemed harder to maintain a decent buzz.

"So, what do you know about those two?" I asked Myra as we waited for the signal at an intersection. There wasn't a car in sight and I felt like an ass waiting to cross.

"Not a lot. We all moved in separately. I don't really know them all that well."

"Did Sean and John know each other before they moved in?" The walk sign lit and we began to cross.

"I don't think so."

"How long have they lived there?"

"I'd guess about four, five months."

"And how long have they been hanging around together?"

"Maybe about the last two months." Myra smiled, as if catching the drift of my questions. "It happened all of a sudden, like overnight."

"Anything else you can think of—odd things, I mean?"

Myra stopped and turned to me. She had a sheepish but earnest look on her face, as if what she wanted to tell me was bit awkward.

"Well... someone's been shitting in the backyard. I think its John or Sean."

"Weird."

We continued walking to the store. My head was swimming with duffle bags, baby hands and yard-shit. I needed a drink, or a smoke. Night had fallen and there was a murky pink haze in the air.

As we walked, we passed an alley. Standing in the shadows was a tall, thin, ghostly pale man. His eyes were wide and vacant, but they followed our every move.

As we passed he whispered, "Ready for the shit to fly, Cal?" His voice was raspy and dry.

He knew me. Word traveled fast among the dead.

"Not just yet, thank you," I tossed back as we passed. I heard him snicker. He liked my joke.

As we were about to turn the corner, the guy yelled after me as if he forgot something, "Somebody came around looking for you!"

I stopped and turned. "Yeah? Who?"

The dead man shrugged.

I flipped him off and kept walking.

Myra was staring again. "What was that?"

I smiled. "A ghoul. Pretty harmless, really. They lurk around, acting creepy."

Myra nodded. She was part of the same generation as me. Raised on TV and movies about vampire lovers, joke-cracking psychos, and little girls possessed by the devil. There was a calm acceptance that isn't found in older folks. "What was that he said?"

"Some ghouls get their jollies taunting the living with stories about a "day of the monsters." They aren't usually superstitious, but they all seem to believe one's coming. There will be nothing but darkness and all the monsters of the world will roam free. Blah, blah, blah. Bunch of bullshit, gives them something to occupy their dried-up brains."

We finally got to a store where the beer was cheap enough to satisfy Myra, so I waited outside while she went in and bought it. I asked her to grab me some smokes and a new lighter. Mine was dead. She was in and out in no time with a case of good, cheap *cerveza*, the kind that didn't give you a hangover, just kept you farting for a week. Fine by me. I offered to carry the case, but she refused.

As we strolled back to the loft, a police car cruised by us slowly. I didn't want to, but I looked over anyway. The cops inside the squad car were clean, slick, and blonde. They checked us out and then moved on. I must've tensed up. Myra noticed.

"You're not a cop, are you?" Myra asked, with suspicion in her voice.

"I was, for about a year. I'm a Private Investigator now."

"What happened?" she walked beside me with a spring in her step, looking me right in my eyes.

"Drug test. I failed with flying colors."

Myra smiled. My slipshod career as a law enforcement officer seemed to have scored me some points. I decided to give it a test run.

"Do you think there's any way you could get John and Sean out of the house? I want to get a look at that basement."

"God, I don't know. Maybe John, but Sean won't even talk to me."

"Forget it. How about just offering them some beer? Maybe distract them and give me a chance to check them out closer."

"Sure, John's a classic freeloader. He'll stampede for free alcohol."

Back at the loft, we put the beer

in the refrigerator and settled into the living area.
Myra showed me some of her artwork. It was
good. The subject matter—hotrods and chicks—
was a bit tired, but she had talent.

I could hear one of the two suspects coughing
in another area of the warehouse. Choking on a
baby, I thought, then dismissed the idea. No use
jumping to conclusions until I knew exactly what
I was dealing with.

On Myra's request, we settled in on the couch
and commenced drinking and smoking. I drank
down two cans of beer in the time she polished
off one. It was the speed. My tolerance was up.
My teeth tingled.

After a while, I heard the coughing again and

this time it was close by. I looked up to see John standing at the entrance to the kitchen area.

"Mind if I grab a beer?" he asked, smiling.

"Help yourself," Myra and I said together.

I turned and winked at her. She giggled and put her hand on my knee.

In the kitchen I heard the fridge open and close, then John coughed, hocked and spit. Lovely.

By the time he came into the room, I needed another beer. He settled into the chair beside the couch as I moved past, into the kitchen. He watched me, smiling like it was the only expression he could muster.

In the kitchen, I grabbed the rest of the six we had started and threw its plastic holder into the trash. That's when I saw where John had spit. And, more importantly, what he'd spit. Spattered against an old carton of milk was a sizeable wad of grayish phlegm. That wasn't strange in itself, but what was mixed in with the slime was: thick black hair, and lots of it.

It seemed John had a hairball.

•   •   •

With suspicions flying like machine gun shells, I walked back to the main room where John and Myra were discussing the rent, something about who owed what. John had produced some Jim Beam (a welcome sight) and offered the bottle to me before my ass had even hit the couch. I took a huge swig that made both of them whistle. I was a little embarrassed, but the whiskey washed it away in seconds.

"So, did Jerry ever show his sorry ass?" John asked, taking a timid swig.

Myra cracked her second beer. "Not unless he came in while we were out."

John shook his head, looking right at me without losing that smile for a single second. "Shitty thing to do. I mean, inviting you, then disappearing."

His grin widened as he finished speaking. There was a black hair stuck in his teeth.

I decided to play it. His cocky attitude was pissing me off.

"You've got something in your teeth," I said.

He didn't react at all. He just plucked the hair from his teeth and flicked it away. "You visiting long?"

Before I could answer, a crash and a quick yell came from downstairs. John and I both jumped to our feet simultaneously. I don't think he knew he was doing it, but he had his hand against my chest to prevent me from moving. When he did realize, he removed his hand. The smile returned instantly.

"Sean is such a klutz. I better go see what he broke."

He moved fast to the service elevator, and then he was gone, into the basement. I needed to get down there. I knew I'd find all the proof I needed to figure out exactly what the hell they were up to and nail these fuckers.

I turned and looked at Myra.

"I think it might be a good idea for you to get out of here," I warned.

She shook her head. "I'm staying right here."

"I thought you had a date."

"I lost interest." She smirked just enough to turn my beaten old face red, then came up to me and put her hand on my cheek.

She started to lean towards me, eyes beginning to close slightly. All of a sudden there was a buzz in the air. She had been flirting with me the whole time and I hadn't even noticed. Now, as she moved towards me, all I could do was stand there like a lug and stare. But before we could connect, the elevator started coming back up. I was shaking, and it had nothing to do with danger.

Peril I could take. Women made me shiver.

Myra and I stepped apart as the elevator opened and John came out. He had a scratch on his cheek. It was light, but I could see four jagged red lines and the glistening of wet blood. John had been clawed by something. I tensed up, knowing things were about to get bad.

John didn't walk over to us; keeping his distance instead. He just stood there with the fake smile all but gone. He had a dreamy, disoriented look about him, like he was drugged or suddenly overcome with fever. He mumbled something about beer and suddenly walked into the kitchen. I gave Myra the silent "scram" signal, but she wasn't having any of it. She had no idea what we were dealing with. To tell the truth, neither did I, but I had my guesses. None of them were good.

"Myra, could you give me a hand?"

It was John calling from the kitchen. His voice was different. In fact it seemed to change as he spoke. It went from normal to a low grumble in mid-sentence.

I shook my head at Myra, but she shook hers right back. "It's okay," and she left the room before I could stop her.

I don't know what was wrong with me. Maybe the new surroundings threw me off my game. I couldn't get my bearings on the situation. I felt trapped and exposed. I was acting like a guest in someone's house even though there was danger in the air. I had to force myself into action.

I checked my gun, making sure it was loaded, then tucked it back into my belt as I moved quickly towards the kitchen. The hairs on my arm stood on end.

I halted just outside, jumping across the entryway to get a quick assessment of the situation inside. As I moved past the door, the service elevator behind me went down to the basement on its own. In the kitchen, I saw blood, a huge swelling pool on the floor.

I feared Myra was already dead.

John thought he was fast, but I heard the noises he made—claws clicking on the ground, clothes tearing beneath a growing body. I knew what I was dealing with. John and Sean were motherfucking, baby-eating, friend-murdering, ass-licking, piece-of-shit werewolves!

I ducked back towards the couch and tried to look normal. John came through the door, but he was covered in shadow. I couldn't get a clean look. He was human, but his cloths were ripped. I didn't want him to suspect that I knew so I let out a momentous belch and picked up the bottle of Beam. It seemed to work. He came striding into the room smiling.

Then his clothes began shredding from his body. His hands and feet were already claws and paws.

There was nothing I could do but sit there, holding the bottle dumbly, watching him transform in front of me. He seemed to be in pain, but at the same time getting some kind of orgasmic pleasure out of it. His body twisted, expanded, and contorted as hair sprang from every inch of his now-naked body. His snout pushed out and his ears grew upwards into points. His eyes turned into wide, green-flecked circles and, I swear to God, he still had that fucking annoying, fake smile. That's what made me mad and propelled me into action.

I threw the bottle of whiskey into his face.

It shattered against his snout, whiskey spraying his face and eyes. He let out a deafening howl of agony. I knew Sean would arrive any second, so I leapt at the flailing beast, jumping over the table with my new lighter in hand, and tackled him. We both went down with a brutal crash. His claws raked my back, my skin split, and I felt the warmth of fresh blood wetting my sweatshirt.

Panicked, I jammed the lighter against his head and flicked it. His head burst into flames, like grandma's wig in the fireplace.

He screamed and threw me hard backwards into the wall. I felt a rib bend and snap, and the weight of my gun falling onto me as I flipped backwards.

Behind me, Sean was coming up the elevator. Above the howls of the flailing, burning werewolf I could hear him barking impatiently inside the cage. I leapt to my feet and tried to stop the elevator, but it was useless. The controls were somewhere else. All I could do was look down through the mesh and watch as a second, larger werewolf came up to the floor.

I ran, jumping over the flaming monster, and grabbed a chair. Before Sean could open the elevator gate, I jammed the chair legs into the mesh on both sides of the gate. He crashed against the meshed steel from the other side and howled. His weight bent the steel door, popping ancient rivets from their sockets and splintering flecks of paint. He was fucking huge. The chair would hold him inside the cage for a minute, tops. I had to get the hell out of there.

Suddenly, John grabbed me from behind and raked his claws across my cheek. I reeled around. He was still on fire, swinging blind. His eyes were seared shut, welded by melted flesh and fur. He howled. I made my move and shoved the gun into his mouth, pulling the trigger again and again until I heard only empty clicks. John was on the floor twitching and bleeding. The back of his wolf-like head was gone.

Everything was moving fast. My back was to the elevator door. Sean was beating it down, pounding the thick mesh apart one powerful blow at a time. I scanned the room for anything to use as a weapon, but I was panicked and bleeding badly. I didn't need anything in particular, no silver bullets or wolf's-head cane. All those myths were total bullshit. I just needed something sharp, flammable, or blunt to bash its skull in.

I ran into the kitchen and my worst fears were confirmed. Myra was dead, sprawled on the floor. Her throat had been viciously removed, her face frozen in her last second of life. Her eyes were wide, mouth agape. She saw her killer before he scratched out her windpipe.

I hardly had time to react as Sean's clawed, red-haired fist came smashing through the steel mesh of the antique elevator. My gun was empty. I was out of options, so I ran for the stairs and out into the streets. Cowardly maybe, but until I had a plan or some kind of weapon, it was my only choice.

It didn't buy me much time, though. Sean was big, fast, and angry, and he was on my ass in no time flat. All werewolves are so fucking angry. That's why I hate dealing with them. Of all creatures, they're the most unreasonable. There's just no talking to them.

I knew I didn't have time to get into my car, and I wasn't about to let that big red freak have at my slick paint job, so I bolted down the desolate street towards what I now recognized as the Staples Center. Maybe if we hit a populated area he'd give up and turn around. I paused and looked behind me. At the end of the street, right next to the Catalina, a huge red wolf stood on hind legs. I also noticed a piece of paper on my windshield. If I got a ticket I'd really be pissed.

Sean came straight at me. I had about a hundred yards on him, but he was fast as shit. When he dropped on all fours he could probably outrace a car. I didn't wait to find out if my guess was right. I bolted toward the intersection where Myra and I had stood only an hour earlier. Traffic had picked up considerably. Maybe I could get him hit by a car.

I kept right on running. Suddenly, people were everywhere. A stadium event must have let out, changing the ghost town into a mob scene. Traffic was heavy, but I didn't slow down—not even slightly. I ran right into the intersection with Sean, nailed to my butt. Unfortunately, the plan (if you could call it that) didn't go quite as well as I'd hoped.

I got mowed down as soon as I hit the street, rolling over a car's hood and flying through the air like a scarecrow shot out of a cannon. Horns and brakes blared, but above it all, I heard the howling cry of the werewolf as he leapt after my rag-doll body. There was chaos, people screaming, and yelling out in confused terror. I lifted my head and there he was, the biggest fucking werewolf I'd ever seen. He was poised over me, arm raised, about to slash me open.

There was nothing I could do. I was dead meat.

Then another car ran me over, hitting Sean too. I guess you could call it one of those good/bad things. I felt the tires roll over my legs. It was fast, but it still hurt like a bitch. I heard Sean howl as the car dragged him into the intersection. Another car came screaming out of nowhere, smashing him between it and the first car.

As I crawled to my feet, the huge, red-haired werewolf ripped the hood off the first car with a single stroke and threw it into the windshield like a massive, deadly Frisbee. The hood shattered the glass, decapitating the two people inside. It all happened so fast I hardly had a chance to react. Bedlam and blood engulfed the street.

To make matters worse, Sean-wolf was still alive and madder than hell. He turned away from the smoldering wreckage and glared right at me. His stare bore into me, human eyes bizarrely pierced through the animal features. He wanted to be sure I saw what he did next. He effortlessly lifted and threw aside the offending car with its headless passengers. I watched dumbly as the car tumbled over the curb to the sidewalk like a crushed beer can.

I weighed my options again, and once more decided to run like hell. I was surprised I could even move. I was covered with blood, my back stung, my chest ached with every stride, and I could hear Sean closing in behind me. His breathing was a loud, angry rasp.

Up ahead a few yards, I spied the alleyway where the ghoul had been standing earlier. He was still there, this time gesturing for me to come. At first I thought he was fucking with me, but then he spoke.

"This way, Cal," he rasped. "This way."

I ran into the alley, moving so fast that I hardly saw the ghoul's creepy grin as I passed. "Thanks," I panted. "What's your name?"

"Emek."

"I owe you."

The end of the alley divided into three directions, so I stopped running and turned. What I saw was unbelievable. Emek was on top of the werewolf's head, with his arms and legs wrapped all the way around the spinning beast's face. But that wasn't the best part. My new pal Emek was laughing, flailing one arm high like he was busting a bronco.

It lasted all of thirty seconds.

The werewolf ripped the ghoul off his head and slammed him to the pavement. Then, with a series of lightning-fast swipes, he ripped Emek's torso to ribbons. Throughout the thrashing, the ghoul kept laughing.

I managed a smile, and then ran to the right. What I knew, and what the Sean-wolf clearly didn't, was that you can't kill a ghoul. At least not that way. They're undead, for Christ's sake! Maybe Emek had bought me a little time. I ran and ran. The pain in my legs was terrible and I was praying I hadn't broken them. Either way, I'd need a hospital if I got out of this.

Any hopes of escape were quickly dashed as I rounded the next turn. I learned the hard way that some LA alleys are dead-ends. Not only was Sean mere feet behind me and closing, but I was running straight toward a tall wooden-plank fence that was way too high to jump or climb. Sean's claws scraped my shoulder, and I felt his breath at the back of my neck.

This was it, I thought. This is how I'd die.

I had one chance, and I took it. I jumped, throwing myself *into* the fence as high and close to the center of the timbers as I could. I hit the fence sideways in a ball and felt the wood splinter on impact. The broken boards flipped backward, pointing behind me as I'd hoped, and exploded into a mass of pointed shards.

Rolling, I heard the sounds I'd prayed for: a hard impact followed by the gurgling of the Sean-wolf impaled on the broken fence.

I hit the ground and leapt to my feet, but immediately fell again. I couldn't get up. I was a mess, but at least I was alive. Sometimes the best plans come out of sheer panic.

Not five feet from me was Sean, human again, impaled on a dozen broken planks of wood. He was still alive, just barely. He craned his head up toward me as I used a trash can to help me to my feet. Blood was pouring from his mouth and one eye was gone. The socket bled freely.

His one eye looked pathetic and sad, as though he wanted to say something to me. Whether it was "fuck you" or "thank you," I couldn't tell. Frankly, I didn't care.

"Tough luck, dog-boy," I said, hobbling away as the cops showed up on the scene.

chapter

 12

The hospital was nice about the

whole thing. Hospitals generally like me. I give them lots of business and tell them stories they don't believe. They patched me up, pumped me full of dope, and handed me to the cops. The LAPD were a different matter, but for the same reasons; they don't like my stories *or* my business. They grilled me for hours and hours even though I was in a deep Morphine haze. I told them the story—the truth—over and over. Of course, they didn't believe a word, but finally one of the little geniuses sent a car over to the loft.

They found what I'd described—as well as the body of Jerry Gallagher in the freezer—with pieces of several others. They found John's body outside the kitchen door and enough evidence to link John and Sean to a long series of murders dating back a couple of months. Evidently, there had been a sudden spike of missing persons in the downtown area and from nearby hospitals. The thefts were Sean and John's attempt to lay low. Eventually, though, their bloodlust got the better of them and they started attacking people on the street.

There was only one part of my story that didn't check out. The cops found blood in the kitchen, but they didn't say anything about Myra's body.

No Myra.

I could only guess what had happened to her. Probably nothing good. Whatever the case, she was out of my hands now. Probably long gone. In a way, if she did turn into one of those things, I was happy for her. At least she was alive. I liked her. I'd hate for her to have died that way.

The LAPD were kind enough to let me go at four a.m. with their usual warning to get a real job. They warned that if I wanted to operate in Los Angeles I'd better get the proper license. Fuck them. Where the hell do you get a license for what I do anyway? Idiots.

I drove back to Sam's place feeling every slice and break on my body. Total: two hundred plus stitches, a broken rib, twisted ankle, and bruises the size of footballs everywhere. Overall, I'd say I was damn lucky to be alive. And my pay for all this was one big-ass zero.

I was glad to be back at Sam's. It was cozy, in a pathetic, disgusting sort of way. There was beer in the fridge, whiskey on the desk and an answering machine full of angry bill collectors that I didn't have to worry about because, for once, they weren't after me. I shed my clothes, shredded and crunchy with dried blood, and took a long shower.

When I came out, she was waiting for me in the living room.

Myra squatted, snarling at me in her wolf form. She must have followed me. She was small and still feminine, but mean looking, with glaring red eyes that didn't blink. Her claws extended and retracted over and over.

I tried to talk to her, to calm her down and tell her we didn't have to do it this way, but she was gone. Her eyes showed no sign of recognition.

I backed away slowly, but with every step I took she advanced two. She was so close that I could feel her hot breath on me.

"Myra," I whispered, "Walk away. Don't do this."

The she-wolf just growled.

I was fucked for the second time in a night. I kept backing away, but she kept coming. Soon, my back was against a wall with nothing in reach.

I slugged her as hard and fast as I could. She wasn't expecting that, and she reeled backwards, losing her balance. I did it again. This time I caught her right in the snout, and she yelped and swiped at my chest, catching a bit of skin. Before she recovered I grabbed the desk chair and smashed it across her head.

She was down, and hurting, so I hit her again, then again, until all I was holding were two splintered chair legs.

I paused, for too long. She was up and coming at me with murder in her animal eyes. I grabbed the whiskey bottle off Sam's desk and smacked it across her face. It shattered, spraying her with burning liquid. It was the second werewolf in one night that I'd downed with whiskey, but shit, you've gotta stick with what works.

Myra was blinded, taking swipes at me and wailing like a wounded dog. I had precious little energy left, and had to think fast. I was staying just out of her reach. She was temporarily blinded, but her vision was clearing fast. Soon she'd have me. I began to make noises as I moved. She followed, flailing at the air without result. Finally, I had her in place. I took one of the shattered chair legs and rammed it through her heart.

She stumbled backwards, blood spouting like a fountain from the hole in her chest. By the time she hit the floor she was dead, and human.

I was too tired to think. Simultaneously, I dialed for the police and dug for another hit of speed, since it looked like I was going to be spending what was left of the night chatting with the LAPD boys yet again. But as the phone rang, something began to happen. Myra's body smoked and sizzled like hot bacon on the floor.

"LAPD. What's your emergency?"

I hung up and watched as Myra's body sizzled down to a bubbling mass, then to ash. Within a minute she was gone. Sometimes that happens. I don't know why.

chapter

1 3

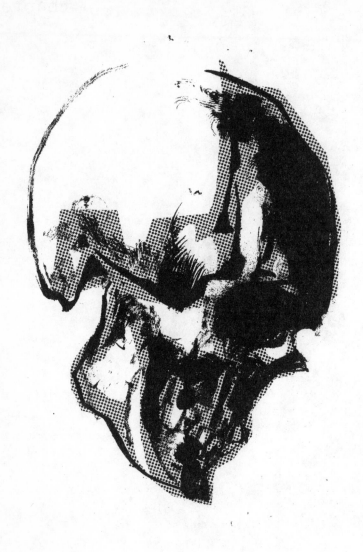

Three days passed without Sam's head

arriving in the mail. I spent the entire time in a drunken, alcohol-and-painkillers induced stupor. I felt like shit. My wounds ached and had me worried. Any number of things can happen when a lycanthrope gets their paws on you. Usually you die. Sometimes you turn into one of them, sometimes you go crazy from a weird fever with rabies-like symptoms. I'd caught the wounds pretty early and had the nurse at the hospital pump me with antibiotics. I just had to keep an eye on the bites and scratches and hope I didn't suddenly develop a craving for Alpo.

I kept thinking about Myra leaning in to kiss me, then a couple hours later lurching forward to kill me. How fucked up was that? It seemed I'd traveled across the country to live the same screwed-up life I always had. I guess I was a fool to think it would be any different, but deep inside, I'd hoped for more.

And though I tried not to think about it too much, the absence of Sam's head had me more than a little tweaked. I had the address of the kid who separated Sam from his body, but I didn't want to risk anything without having the head, too. The downside was that the kid had more time to do whatever the fuck he wanted with the body.

I'd woken up around three that afternoon with a massive headache. I wanted nothing less than absolute quiet as I attempted to pull my head up from the couch. I had to be slow and careful getting up, lest I make noise and send my brain into a spiral of pain. I eased my stiff and sore body over the edge of the couch until my feet were near the floor. I didn't dare open my eyes. My eggshell skull barely contained my rattled brain.

Had I thought about it, I would have remembered the floor was covered with cans and bottles. My feet hitting the ground sounded like a garbage truck dumping its load. I screamed, eyes shooting open. I was dead center in a room of pain.

"Fuck! Fuck! Fuck! Fuck! Fuck!"

Somehow I made it to the bathroom, where I swallowed any pills that gave promise of relief, and then sat on the toilet until it was dark again. I drank the remains of a beer I found on the floor next to the shower and after a while I started to feel better.

I threw up. Felt even better.

I walked into the kitchen and grabbed what was left in the Mr. Coffee and drank it straight from the pot, realizing too late that I hadn't made coffee since I'd arrived. With my last gulp, I felt something solid slide down my throat.

I needed some time to recover. It had only been a few days since the werewolf debacle and I was still suffering badly. Half of my stitches had gotten infected. The wounds throbbed constantly, no matter what I put on them or how they were dressed.

Some downtime was just what the doctor ordered. But my life just never seems to work that way. Things were about to get back to the bizarre.

Outside the house, someone was leaning on their car horn. I tried to ignore it. I laid back down and covered my head with a pillow, but nothing would make that fucking sound stop. Finally, I grabbed the .45 and marched out the front door, ready to shoot the person in the car right through the fucking eye.

But it wasn't a person, and it wasn't a car. It was a U-Haul truck with a ghoul driver. I knew him. It was Mo'Lock.

A wide smile spread across my face. I couldn't help it. I put the gun away and walked toward the curb as he climbed out of the truck's cab.

"What the hell are you doing, you crazy fucking ghoul?!"

Mo'Lock grabbed me by my shoulders. The corners of his mouth curled ever so slightly, which for the undead was a sign of almost total joy.

"I got your message," Mo'Lock said. "From Simon. I packed your stuff and drove out here as fast as I could."

I ignored him and pointed at the U-Haul. "That's my stuff?"

"Everything you left behind."

"Where the hell were you? I looked everywhere for you before I left," I said, the slightest hint of aggravation in my voice.

The ghoul looked sheepish. "New Jersey."

"New Jersey?!" I hit myself in the head. "What the fuck is in New Jersey?!"

The ghoul walked away without answering and opened the back of the truck. The back was loaded with all of my crap, every last little scrap of paper I'd left behind. He'd even packed the rotten food from the kitchen and the trash from my office waste basket. Stupid ghoul.

We got the truck unpacked pretty quickly. It soon became clear just how alike Sam and I were: the house now had two desks, two pairs of filing cabinets, two couches and so on. We had double loser supplies.

As we emptied the last load, I looked up the street and saw Benito and his pals. They waved at me. I waved back. Then I spotted a large figure walking up the sidewalk toward the house. It was Emek, the ghoul who'd helped me out with the wolf-boy.

Mo'Lock looked at the approaching ghoul. "Who's that?"

"Emek. He's cool."

"He's undead."

I winked at Mo'Lock. "Jealous?"

Emek walked up to us, stopped and stood silent before us, a living corpse. His posture gave the appearance of a loosely dangling marionette. He was shorter than Mo'Lock by a foot and had light, close-cut hair. There was a lonely quality about him that surprised me. Ghouls back East are pretty social. They don't have much to do with the living, but they interact with each other quite a bit.

Emek looked nervous. You don't see this much with the dead. When you do, it usually means trouble.

I introduced him to Mo'Lock and they exchanged undead pleasantries in a babbling mish-mash of English spoken at a superhuman rate. I figured they were comparing notes on undead life on the East versus the West.

Emek's nervousness set me on edge. But he'd saved my sorry ass, so I'd hear him out, if the two ghouls ever decided to shut up. I broke up the chat and invited them both into the house. As we walked to the front door, both ghouls looked at the grassless yard with the huge grooves gouged into the yard.

"Nice lawn," Mo'Lock said.

I told him to fuck off and pushed him into the house. It was good to see the stupid fucking ghoul.

●　　●　　●

"So what's up?" I asked Emek. "Speak to me."

I was sitting on Sam's couch. Mo'Lock stood near the window, eyeing the new ghoul with a suspicion I'd never seen in him before. His entire stance was rigid and stand-offish, so Emek lingered awkwardly near the door. Ghouls always preferred to stand. Again, I don't know why. They're a mysterious bunch.

Emek's eyes were wide, like those fucking awful paintings my grandmother had an overzealous affinity for: those doe-eyed punks with flowers and puppies. His teeth were tight together, pale lips parted as though he was freezing to death.

Finally, he spoke. "Cal McDonald," he said, "I've come to warn you."

I glanced over at Mo'Lock and bit my nails.

"Warn me?" I lit a cigarette and tossed the match.

"There's a guy in town. He heard you were here and what you've done," Emek stammered. "Now he's looking for you."

The new ghoul was really agitated. His palpable fear freaked me out more than the warning.

I let his words sink in, flicked my ashes on the floor, took a nip of whiskey and looked from one ghoul to the other.

"And?" I said in a bored voice.

Mo'Lock moved around to the side of the couch. "How does anyone know that Cal is in Los Angeles?"

Emek looked at Mo'Lock. "Word is out. Everybody knows."

I leaned back in the couch. "I'm a fucking celebrity."

"Not exactly," Emek said, looking around the room. The whites of his eyes almost eclipsed the tiny black specks of his pupils. If he had irises, I couldn't seem them. Those pin-prick pupils dug right into me, and my cigarette dropped from my lips. Something in his tone got my heart going. There was weirdness in the air. I couldn't put my finger on it, but something was definitely wrong.

I picked up my smoke. When I sat back up, he was looking at me with the same stare. He hadn't flinched.

"You don't get it," Emek said. "This guy's very bad news. He's been running the LA underworld for a long time."

"He some kind of magic type?" I was in no mood. The pain in my wounds was really coming on strong. I had a scrape on my shoulder that stung like a bitch.

The ghoul leaned forward. "No. He's a vampire. The biggest, meanest, and oldest one ever. No one's even seen him for over fifteen years. He doesn't need to hunt anymore. He's got things that do that for him. The only time he surfaces is when he's got some score to settle. It seems he's picked you. If I was you, I'd be worried."

"I am," I yawned. "I'm very, very worried. What's this big shit's name?"

"David."

"The vampire's name is Dave?"

"Well... um... yeah."

I glared at the ghoul. "That's not the most fear-inspiring name I've ever heard. Yours scares me more."

Even Mo'Lock let out a little breathy laugh. I shot Mo' a look and wink.

Emek suddenly slapped his hand on the coffee table, agitated. "I didn't name him! The point is, this guy's after you. Word has it he's holed up at the old Houdini House in Coldwater Canyon."

"What's he gonna do, saw me in half?"

"You do what you want. We're even now." He turned and stomped toward the door. "Good luck."

I stood up. "Whoa, whoa, whoa. Hold up there, Emek."

The ghoul stopped at the door, upset. He thought I wasn't taking him seriously and thereby disrespecting him. I put my hand on his shoulders.

"Look, I wasn't taking any shots at you," I told him. "I've dealt with a lot of these freaks before, so I make fun. That's all."

Emek nodded. "Let me ask you this, Cal. When was the last time you dealt with werewolves and vampires in the same week?"

I looked at Mo'Lock and we both shrugged. The new ghoul had me there. That was pretty weird. I deal with a lot of shit compared to the normal world, but authentic cases of the supernatural are pretty few and far between, even for me.

"Look," I said, "I'll check this Dave shmuck out and see what his beef is, okay?"

Emek pointed at his sunken eyes. "Look at everything differently. Something is in the air."

"Uh, ok."

With that he was gone. Mo'Lock and I stood in the door and watched him walk out of the gate, past the U-Haul, and down the sidewalk.

It wasn't that I didn't take Emek's warning to heart—I did believe him. I just wasn't scared. I was too distracted by the pain of my wounds. I lifted my shirt to look at one of the bigger ones on my chest. It was definitely healing; there was no discoloration. It just throbbed.

Mo'Lock made a disgusted face. "You should have those looked at."

I vowed to go to the doctor if it didn't feel better in a week or two. At the moment, I had to get myself psyched about this Dave fellow. This vampire.

I could sit and wait for him to come after me, or go get him. Both choices seemed a little stupid, for different reasons. Waiting was boring—I'd had my fill of that, wasting time until Sam's head arrived. But going after him meant I was sure to get into a scrap, and I didn't really feel like putting my body through any more punishment just yet. Fortunately, I was now a bit more prepared for vampires since Mo'Lock had been kind enough to lug my shit cross-country.

In one of the boxes, among piles of papers and back issues of *Speculator*

Magazine, there was a cigar box filled with my vampire-killing supplies. I sat at Sam's desk and examined the contents.

Inside was your standard Holy Cross and its companion vial of Holy Water, along with two wooden stakes and a Star of David to use against the rare, but deadly, Jewish vampire. The real reason I dug the box out, though, was six custom-made hardwood .38 caliber bullets.

I'd had them made about a year ago, after a couple of strutting jackass vampires were running around the Mall killing off tourists. I killed them with stakes, but what a pain in the ass! Most vampires have a tendency to wake up before the stake's all the way in, which kind of upsets them. They get hopping mad and start fighting back. That's exactly what happened, so I had to forget the stakes and go to Plan B. I burned one and hacked the other with an ax. It was a big fucking mess. By the time I'd downed them, I'd broken both my legs and one of my arms in three places. No fucking way I was going through that again: hence, the wooden bullets.

Just for the record, you don't *need* wooden bullets to stop a vampire. I've killed some with straight-up lead ammo. Shit, I killed one with a hammer! But it takes almost fifty shots to blow enough holes in them to overwhelm their weird immune system. Wooden bullets don't burn the flesh, so the holes stay open and they bleed out faster.

Mo'Lock watched me while I loaded the bullets into the .38.

"Is that safe?"

"Probably not."

The ghoul moved to the other side of the room and looked out the front window. He narrowed his eyes and scanned the yard and beyond.

"You know this neighborhood is overrun by vampires already?"

"Yeah," I said, "I talked to them. They're cool."

"Cool vampires?"

I shrugged. "What can I say? They came over, introduced themselves. They were nice."

Mo'Lock nodded. He was impressed. "This Los Angeles is an interesting place."

I was packed and ready to go. "I guess," I said as I walked towards the door. "You coming?"

"You want me to come?"

I stared at him for a good thirty seconds, then walked out the door. I wasn't gonna put up with any sensitive, whiny crap. He was trying to make me feel guilty for ditching him in DC. Against my better instincts, I glanced over my shoulder as I reached the Catalina. Mo'Lock was standing in the window like rejected puppy. I almost felt bad for him. Fucking ghoul.

I flipped him off with a smile, climbed in my car and sped away. I had me a vampire to shoot.

It was a nice night for a drive,

considering I was on my way to kill a blood-sucker. I tried to take my time, but the Houdini house was near Sam's. A quick drive over a steep, winding hill put me at the house twenty minutes after I'd left. I'd swallowed a handful of painkillers so my head was a bit light. My teeth were numb and loose, and all my wounds throbbed. I'm not one to complain, but those things were itching like they were trying to win a fucking contest.

I scanned the Houdini house. Like many houses in LA, it was huge and crammed into the side of a hill. The driveway looked more like an obstacle course than a place to leave a car. I parked at the bottom and walked up as I cased the joint. Based on the map, I was less then a half a mile from Sunset Boulevard, but I might as well have been in the backwoods of West Virginia. There was no traffic, and besides the Houdini house all I could see were trees.

I snooped around the side of the huge Spanish-style house, looking for a way in. All of the windows were boarded up, even on the upper floors. Classic vampire scenario. Finally, as I moved around toward the back of the house, I found a window that hadn't been boarded shut. It was pitch black inside, but I hoisted myself onto the sill and slid into the house anyway.

The place was a wreck and stunk of piss and vomit. I stood there a second, waiting for my eyes to adjust, when something very odd happened. I heard a small noise. Nothing bad, just a creak. My heart jumped ever so slightly—nothing weird about that. But all my wounds started pulsating, as if reacting to the fear. *That* shit was a little too weird, even for me.

My eyes adjusted enough so that I could make my way around. The room I was standing in must have been some kind of game room. The walls were lined with dusty, padded benches, slashed and spilling their stuffing. In the center of the room was the remains of a red velvet-topped pool table. From the looks of it now, it was used primarily as a toilet. There were turds all over the torn velvet top and even a small pile in one of the corner pockets.

I've seen a lot of weird things in my life, but the idea of a vampire climbing up on a table to take a dump was beyond my comprehension. Wouldn't it just be easier to use the floor? But, I had to admit, the turd in the corner pocket was pretty funny. Vampires like to come off like they're better then anyone else, but they crap just like you and me if they eat. With all this fecal matter, I guess ol' Dave liked to chew his victims as well as suck them.

I moved into the next room and down a long corridor towards the front of the house. As I neared the end of the hall, I stopped. There was a door just ahead of me with light, dim and flickering, seeping beneath it. Bingo. The light was from a small fire, probably a candle. Big shot Dave was probably having his morning tea at his grand piano by candlelight. Vampires are such hoity-toity jerk-offs. They all think they're some kind of aristocrats or some shit. I was looking forward to shooting him.

I decided against luring him out. Just lunging into the room shooting seemed like much more fun. I took out my .38 with the hardwood slugs and carefully grabbed the knob. I listened for a second. All was quiet. At my feet, the candlelight flickered, licking at the tips of my shoes.

Using my uninjured shoulder, I pushed the door open and stepped quickly inside. Everything slowed as adrenaline flooded my system and I scanned the room for my target. He was there, on the other side of the small dusty room, lankly and deathly pale. He was shorter than I imagined, but it had to be him.

He was more than a bit surprised to see me. His black-circled eyes were wide as dinner plates, thin brows arched cartoon-like to his greasy hairline. His skin was a smooth, eggshell-white. I stepped forward, he stepped backwards, and neither of us said a word. That was fine by me. I hate deathbed monologues.

I raised my gun nice and slow until it was leveled at his heart. The vampire tried to keep backing away, but a casket was in the way. I stepped forward and closed the space between us until I was just out of his reach. "Say goodnight, *Dave.*"

The vampire stammered. "I... I... I'm—" was all I let him get out.

I let loose with the wooden bullets at close range, unloading the gun into his chest. Blamm! Blamm! Blamm! Blamm! Blamm! Blamm! It was beautiful. He was too busy gurgling and flailing as his chest exploded to even attempt an attack. It was bloody, but quick.

And way too easy.

"What he was trying to tell you...," said a voice behind me.

My heart jumped. My wounds throbbed. I swung around, holding my empty, smoking gun. There was huge shape standing in the doorway.

"...was that he wasn't David."

Standing at the door, blocking the only way out, was the biggest, ugliest motherfucker I'd ever seen in my life. He was leaning casually against the door frame, baring his fangs and tapping his long white fingers on his thigh. "You just shot my manservant."

Son-of-a-bitch.

•   •   •

I was so screwed. I'd used up all of my bullets on some poor, bug-eating, vampire manservant, and now I was face-to-face with probably the biggest undead goon I'd ever seen. If I was going to survive, I'd have to use my wits.

"I don't suppose saying sorry would help?"

The vampire shook his head slowly.

I gave the situation considerable thought in the time it took my stomach to sink to my knees, then bum-rushed him. The cocky sumbitch wasn't expecting the attack at all, so I hit him dead in the chest with all my weight. We both flew

backwards. Our combined weight must have been over four hundred pounds,
so we went right through the wall behind him in a cloud of plaster dust and
termite-infested wood.

He wasted no time, using a leg thrust against my chest to vault me across the
room like a wet rag. The bastard was strong. I slammed into the casket on the
other side of the room and fell in a heap. It hurt. Hurt bad.

The casket tumbled over. Soil from inside scattered all over me, the floor, and
the bleeding corpse of his servant. By the time I looked up from my blood-mud
bath, Dave was standing over me.

My wounds were burning, as if my body was suddenly a massive beating
heart on speed. Each infected laceration felt about to rip open at any second.

I scrambled clumsily to my knees and grabbed hold of two slats of broken
wood. Dave was behind me, so I didn't try to stand. Instead, I spun around,
holding the pieces together to form a cross. The big bloodsucker stopped short,
hissed and reeled away. It worked. He really *was* old. Only Old World, fallen-
Christian type vampires were scared of crosses.

I got to my feet, keeping the slats crossed and out in front of me. I maneu-
vered around, keeping Dave at a distance. He was hissing at me and baring his
fangs, putting on a big old dramatic show. Tiny flecks of foam curdled at the
corners of his mouth and from his small upturned nose.

"Okay, here's the deal," I said. "I'd like to leave here in one piece, so I want
you to give me a little head start."

He glared at me and hissed. "I'll get you now or I'll get you later. I can wait.
I've got all the time in the world."

He put down his arms and closed his mouth.

I slowly backed out of the room the way I had come, keeping my eyes
locked on his until I was out. I waited outside the door a second to see if he'd
try to follow me. Nothing happened. I think the appeal of getting me later
stopped him. Whatever the case, I turned and bolted for the window. I leapt
through it, ripping my jacket as I did. I got up fast, trying to ignore the pain, and
continued running until I got back to the car.

Before driving off I glanced up at the house. In one of the windows I could
see the shape of the vampire watching me, backlit by the flickering light of the
candle. Dramatic asshole.

Round one was over.

1 5

I drove back over the hill to Sam's

house via the back streets of Studio City. When I
passed Benito and his crew standing outside one
of their houses, I noticed they had a barbecue
going. Wives, kids and family were milling in the
yard. As I drove by, Benito gave me a nod and
waved his roasting fork towards me. I nodded
back and smiled. He had on an apron that read
"Make Mine Rare".

I parked at the curb. As soon as the door
closed I heard a light, airy, clicking sound. I
turned. At first I didn't see anything, and then

behind a car at the end of the block I spied a brand-new red VW Beetle. The dealer sticker was still in the back window. The driver's side window was open and someone inside had just lowered something. Since I wasn't shot, my guess was a camera.

I pretended not to see anything and began walking into the house, but at the gate I abruptly turned and ran at the Beetle. The driver jumped, scared, and tried to start the car, but I was at the window before the engine sparked. The driver froze as I grabbed the door. It was a woman. She was young looking, with dirty blonde hair and the largest almond-shaped blue eyes I'd ever seen. She was beautiful.

"What are you doing?" I said a bit too loud. My voice cracked at the end.

I expected denial, mace in the eyes, or at least some indignant anger, but instead she turned red, looked at me and then stared down at the steering wheel. I'd seen this before, just not towards me. It was the way a fan acted.

"You *are* Cal McDonald right?" she asked.

I had rushed the car pissed and ready to kill. Now, suddenly I was flustered. I could feel my own face flushing red. "Yeah. Yes. I am. Who are you?"

She flashed her blue eyes at me and smiled. "Sabrina Lynch. *Speculator Magazine.*"

I stared at her. Sabrina Lynch. The name rattled my brain. She worked for the rag that ran pictures of me naked and covered with pink slime, the magazine that called me DC's crackpot detective, the one that had once accused me of taking money for fake ghost-chasing jobs (true, but beside the point). It was also the magazine which featured my old cop buddy, Jefferson Blout, on the cover after the second Big Head case. Blout was so embarrassed, he hasn't spoken to me since.

I let go of the door and backed away from the car. Suddenly she wasn't looking so cute and that flirtatious look on her face seemed more like a wise-ass smirk.

"Any comment for our readers about why you're in Los Angeles? Can you shed some light on the disappearance of Sam Burnett?"

I didn't say a word. I turned away and walked back to the house. I heard her snap one more picture and then drive away. Bitch.

◆   ◆   ◆

Back at Sam's, I stood in front of the bathroom mirror with my shirt off and studied my wounds. It was very strange. They had stopped stinging the moment I was safe, almost the exact second I was clear of the vampire, as though they were in sync with my emotions.

I poked at a nasty gash running over my left shoulder and half-way down my back. A werewolf—Sean, I think—had gotten me from behind when I was running. The wound was deep and infected. The slash across my right cheek was almost completely gone. A little pink, but that was it. But back at the Houdini house it had throbbed as vigorously as the fresher wounds.

I wasn't too worried about the vampire attacking anytime soon. I'd only left him an hour ago, and I was sure he thought I was sweating it out. I did take one precaution, though: I was wearing a cross I'd kept in the box with the bullets. I knew I should be a little more concerned about the Dave situation, but the wound weirdness distracted me. Something about it had me really worried.

Then Mo'Lock appeared at the bathroom door.

"You okay?" he grumbled.

"I thought you were pissed at me."

"I was angry. I came all this way and you left me behind. But I was also worried. Did you kill him?"

I turned and rolled my eyes as I pushed past him into the living room where I grabbed the bottle of Beam. "Well, I killed somebody. It wasn't Dave," I said. "But we did meet."

"What happened?"

"We had a little scrap. That's one pissed off vampire." I took a drink. "But I got away."

Mo'Lock shifted on his feet. "What now?"

I swallowed, choking a little. "I haven't the slightest idea. Just wait, I guess."

Mo'Lock started pacing back and forth in front of me. I sipped the whiskey until he started talking. "I went out for a walk while you were gone. This LA is an interesting place."

"Yeah?"

Something was on his mind. He wasn't very good at concealing his limited emotional range. A little agitation showed on him like a fresh bruise. I waited for him to cough it up.

"I met some fellow ghouls. They are rather lazy. Evidently it's possible to live here without working. But they told me some things which I found rather disturbing."

I yawned and rolled my hand in the air for him to go on.

"They spoke of a coming darkness. The time of the monsters, you know, the floodgate."

"Oh yeah, that. So what?"

"Well... I think it's started. Something or someone has triggered the event. Look around you. Haven't things been stranger than usual since you arrived? You've had steady work!"

"I wouldn't exactly call it work. More like an attack. Is there a point coming soon?"

The ghoul was getting uncharacteristically excited. "I've phoned back East and the same thing is happening there. My brothers and sisters feel it too. Some are so scared they won't even come out of the sewers. They think you're a part of it."

I took a good long drink and then stared at Mo'Lock with the dullest expression I could muster. "Wouldn't I have to know what the fuck you're talking about to be involved?"

Mo'Lock nodded earnestly. He saw that I truly had no idea what he was going on about. I'd heard this kind of talk before and nothing ever came of it.

"It's in the air. I can feel it. Something has been set in motion and it is aimed at you. Something big. Very, very big."

"You're talking shit. You know that, don't you? The only reason I'm getting more *business* is because I'm new here, not because of the coming of some god-damn monster Armageddon. You watch, as soon as we get Sam's head in the mail things will settle down." I took a few swigs and watched Mo'Lock pace, then added, "And what the fuck do ghouls have to be scared of? You're the damn undead, ain't you?"

"Plenty, if it's the right kind of threat. At the core of our being, we are a thing which exists on a spiritual, mystical plane. If that plane is disturbed, we're all in trouble."

"Even the human race?"

"*Especially* the human race."

I thought about it. I'd heard the ghoul go on like this before, but this time there seemed to be some extra weight to his argument. I took a couple of short sips and mulled it over as Mo'Lock watched me. I could feel his big eyes on me, so I looked up at him and met his gaze. "Let's say this shit *is* going on. Is there anything that can be done to stop it?"

He shrugged.

"Then what the fuck are we worrying about it for?"

He shrugged again. "It is a strong feeling, Cal."

"Well, let me know when the feeling gets a little more specific. I've heard all this before and nothing terrible's ever happened."

Mo'Lock looked at me dull-eyed. "Nothing *but* terrible things happen to you."

I raised the bottle to him. Touché.

Then I noticed a pile of mail on the table. To my surprise and dismay, they had my name on them. I picked up an overdue bill from DC, a last notice on a couple of credit cards, then I saw the yellow change of address sticker. I threw down the bills.

"Did you put in a change of address for me?"

Mo'Lock nodded. I laughed. That explained how *Speculator* found me so fast. But I wasn't laughing for long. Poking out from the pile was a small pink slip. I put down the bottle and yanked it out. It was a package delivery slip. It said "Delivery Attempted" and "Final Notice".

"What the fuck?!"

"What is it?"

"It says here they tried to deliver a package twice! Now we have to go to the post office and pick it up because it requires a signature."

"You think it's Mr. Burnett's head?"

"DC zip code."

Mo'Lock snapped his fingers. "Ah, yes. With everything going on I forgot to mention that Brent said he would send Mr. Burnett's head Priority Mail so it would get here as fast as possible."

I rubbed my eyes. "So the first and second delivery attempts probably happened the first few days I was here."

I stood up and quickly fell back into the couch. Painkillers and hooch made for a major head rush. The ghoul stepped over and helped me up. We had to get to the post office.

Mo'Lock followed me out of the house. I got the zipper of my jacket stuck on the screen door, yanked and ripped both my jacket and the door.

"Perhaps I should drive."

"Perhaps you should."

The post office was packed.

The line stretched from the desk, where two of a possible five stations were open, all the way past a wall of P.O. boxes to the back entrance. I stood impatiently with Mo'Lock, gripping the pink slip in my hands while I watched customers take their sweet time at the counter.

As we crawled up the line, I glared at several idiots who evidently had never mailed anything before. They stood at the desk with unpacked boxes begging the clerk to guide them through the complicated process of taping a box closed and putting an address label on it.

Finally it was our turn to stand like retards at the counter while everyone stared at us. Luckily, I had the ghoul with me. He tends to draw most of the attention, and one return glance from him causes most people to look away immediately.

I handed the clerk—who was not a ghoul, but sure as shit looked like one—the pink slip. He looked at it lazily, sighed, and lumbered out of our sight. After a long, silent wait, he shuffled back holding only the pink slip.

"Package is on the truck. Should be delivered today."

"But this says final notice," I said.

The clerk just looked at me and shrugged. I began to reach for my blackjack, but Mo'Lock pulled me away from the counter and out of the post office. The clerk didn't even react. He just yelled, "Next!"

Outside I pushed Mo'Lock off me and composed myself. "Now what? I came here to help that old bastard find his body, but I can't do shit without the head."

"Back to the house and wait for the mailman?"

I stomped off, wounds aching and stinging. I was pissed off. All of a sudden, I had three thousand things on my mind. I had Sam's head case to think about. I was in a new city. Plus, I was being stalked by some broad from a magazine that seemed to like making me look bad. That really fucking ticked me off. I mean, you'd think a magazine that wanted to prove the existence of the supernatural would be nice to the one guy who had first-hand experience!

Maybe the ghouls were right. Maybe something was going on. Something bigger than everybody suddenly jumping on my shit.

Then, out of my anger, I had an idea.

First we drove by Sam's house and left a note for the mailman to leave the package, then we headed out to locate the offices of *Speculator Magazine*. If something was up, if there was one shred of truth in what the ghoul claimed, the magazine should have been tracking an increased amount of bizarre activity. Plus, Ms. Lynch had mentioned Sam. Maybe she had something on the prick bastard who snipped his head from his body.

Finding Sabrina Lynch and the magazine office proved to require some real detective work. The address for the mag led Mo'Lock and me to a post office box. It wasn't an official USPS box, just a service that provides you with a street address. We tried, in vain, to get some info out of the proprietor, but she wouldn't cough up. I tried the white pages, and even called information, but Lynch was unlisted and the magazine phone number was an answering service. Out of sheer desperation, I even put a call in to Sam's Sheriff buddy, Dawson, in Sherman Oaks, but there was no answer.

I was getting frustrated, I refused to give up. I was jittery and needed to keep on the move. I needed the distraction. My entire body stung like a massive paper-cut dipped in rubbing alcohol. I kept throwing back painkillers, but all they did was slur my speech and make my gums throb.

It was in moments like these that my old cravings came back. What I needed was a line of smack to drown out all the noise. I could almost feel the calming haze, but I would never go back to that. I had enough problems without becoming a junkie again.

I remembered the dealer sticker in Lynch's window and, through some miracle of brain-cell survival, I recalled the name at the top of the sticker: Miller/Cruz Volkswagen in North Hollywood. Mo'Lock and I headed deep into the San Fernando Valley to find the dealership. As we ventured further, the ghoul started getting jumpy.

"What's up, Mo'?" I asked as I steered along a vast flat row of what looked like warehouses but were, in fact, stores.

"Look around," the ghoul said. "There's sun everywhere. The only place I see shade is beneath parked cars."

I glanced around as I ran a red light. I hadn't even realized the sun had come up. I'd been up for two days straight. What the ghoul said was true. Somehow the sun beat down so straight and so even that there was little or no place to find shade. It didn't help that there were no trees and all of the buildings were plain gray or brown pillboxes.

After passing under a freeway overpass, we came upon block after block of car dealerships, laid out like graveyards filled with rows of bright, shiny tombstones. I drove slowly by each dealership looking for Miller/Cruz. As we drove past, salesmen gathered, eyeballing us like slobbering zombies waiting for a chance to bite the flesh off the bones. Talk about creepy. I'd rather deal with zombies.

The Miller/Cruz lot was the smallest of all. They seemed to only deal Beetles and had only two salesmen working, neither of whom were named Miller or Cruz. Mo'Lock and I stepped into the showroom and were immediately approached by both men. They introduced themselves as Jon and John and commenced the hard sell. I let them go for about two seconds, then held up my hand.

"You keep pretty detailed records of everybody you sell a car to, right?" Jon looked at John and nodded.

I weighed the options: come back later and break-in, pay off the two J's for info, or distract them while Mo'Lock snoops. I didn't have patience for any of that, so I pulled out my gun and pressed it to Jon's forehead.

"Red Beetle sold to a woman recently. Blonde. Somewhat professional looking. Ring any bells?"

Jon peed himself and nodded. "We've only sold two reds in the last month. One was a dude."

They coughed up the sales info immediately. Just like that I had Sabrina Lynch's address, phone number and bank info. No problem except for the stain in Jon's trousers. I felt bad. The strong arm wasn't necessary at all and more than a little rash, possibly even stupid. If they squealed to the cops I could be traced back through Sabrina Lynch. Luckily, Mo'Lock had some cash on him, so I asked him to give John and Jon five big ones each. That seemed to make everybody happy. Well, except for the ghoul, but fuck him. He'd get over it.

1 7

It turned out that the home

of Sabrina Lynch and the offices of the internationally distributed *Speculator Magazine* were one and the same, and neither was all that impressive. The place was an apartment, one of those "Melrose Place" deals that looked like a small motel with a pool in the middle. But, unlike the TV show, this one had no gorgeous tenants, just a hunchbacked pool boy trying to scoop a beer bottle out of the water with a plastic bag taped to a broom handle.

I checked the mailboxes, found her name, and headed up to apartment six. As we climbed the noisy metal stairs, I looked at the ghoul. He rolled his eyes. I didn't think Los Angeles was agreeing with him.

"What's the matter?" I asked.

"I can't put my finger on it," he said. "Something is wrong... like a cloud following us."

We reached the landing to Lynch's apartment. I stopped and turned to Mo'Lock. "Let me know when you figure it out. In the meantime, shut the fuck up. You're freaking me out."

We proceeded to the door. Inside we could hear all kinds of noise: the TV, a woman's high-pitched voice talking to a pet, a phone ringing. I knocked, and the place went silent. Bang. Just like that. I knocked again. I heard movement, papers ruffling. Panic sounds.

"Just a minute!"

I pounded hard on the door. "IRS! Open up! We've come for the car!"

Silence again, then the door was yanked open, and Sabrina Lynch and I stood face to face. Her hair was pulled back into two small pony-tails. She was wearing sweatpants and a T-shirt which bluntly read "FUCK". I tried not to, but I smiled anyway.

Lynch twisted her lip and smirked. "Not funny and rude. Great combo you got going there, McDonald."

I looked past her, into the apartment, and saw piled papers and clippings scattered everywhere, alongside photos and maps with post-it notes. Where there wasn't furniture, there were stacks of boxes overflowing with back issues of the *Speculator.* The rest of the small apartment was pure function: FAX machine, phones, computer, desk chair, couch and coffee table. The kitchen was a small area against the far wall. There was only one other door; the bathroom I guessed. No bedroom, which explained the sheet and pillow on the couch.

I had all the time in the world to scan her place from the door, because Lynch had finally noticed the ghoul standing behind me. When I looked back to her, her eyes were filled with an odd blend of wonderment and suspicion. She didn't even know I was looking at her. Mo'Lock had her transfixed and it made the ghoul very uncomfortable. I found that hugely amusing.

Finally she looked towards me with dazed eyes. "Is he...?"

I nodded.

"Wow."

Mo'Lock held out his gigantic, bony hand to her. "I'm Mo'Lock. I work with Cal."

Lynch shook his hand and flinched slightly at his cold touch. She smiled so widely I thought her face would tear, and she started to breathe heavy. She was so excited meeting an actual ghoul that she was hyperventilating. But she quickly regained her composure and went from fan to reporter in the blink of an eye.

"So, you tracked me down," she said. "What do you want?"

"Well, we came for a tour of the *Speculator* offices, but I just got one from the door here." I flashed a big fake grin and continued. "And... I wanted to ask you some questions about the Los Angeles scene."

"Like what?"

Mo'Lock leaned in. "May we come inside?"

Lynch jumped and started breathing hard again. I thought she was about to have an anxiety attack. Then, to my surprise, she stepped back and gestured for us to come in.

The wall to the right had a complete publishing schedule for the magazine plastered on it with due dates, ship dates, and a ton of stuff that made no sense to me. I knew there were at least a hundred issues of *Speculator*. It was a slick product. I couldn't believe it was all done from this little rat-hole.

She knew what I was thinking and stepped over to me while Mo'Lock looked around in his odd, slow way.

"I have over a hundred and sixty-five writers and photographers and ten editors scattered all over the world. Most of the work is done over the Internet. There's a large community of investigative reporters interested in the paranormal and only one magazine that will run their stories."

I scanned the schedule. Words popped out; vampire, telepathy and UFOs were a prominent part of the next issue, followed by an all-Bigfoot/Loch Ness Monster Special. Grainy photos were posted on the wall. Most were the familiar ones everybody has seen; the noodle-like head of Nessy sticking out of the water, Bigfoot striding through a clearing, and a close-up of an oversized plaster foot impression.

Then I spotted a post-it with "SHERMAN OAKS CULT" scrawled on it. I pointed to it.

"What's this?"

She eyed me suspiciously. "A tip I received. It didn't pan out. Why?"

"Just curious."

"Sherman Oaks was the last place your buddy Sam Burnett was seen alive."

Mo'Lock pulled himself away from a stack of papers and walked over clearing the apartment in three strides. "How do you know that?"

She looked from Mo'Lock to me and laughed. "Look, you guys want to tell me what you're looking for? I'm not used to people barging in here and asking a bunch of questions!"

"I'm not used to people sneaking pictures of me."

Lynch laughed again and smiled. "Fair enough. I guess I've embarrassed the famous Cal McDonald enough to give you some slack." Her body language relaxed and I could tell in the beat of a heart that she decided to trust us.

"One thing though," she said, holding up a finger.

"Name it."

"If I help you, I get an interview. No holds barred, tell-all."

"Deal."

●   ●   ●

I told Sabrina Lynch about how I came to move to LA, about the head in the box and the kid who separated it from Sam's body. She said she got an anonymous tip about a teen cult in Sherman Oaks, but the lead was thin and she couldn't find anything justifying further investigation. Later she heard about Sam's disappearance. That's when she showed up at his place and saw me.

"I was kind of shocked to see you. I'd run stories and pictures of you so I recognized you immediately as Sam's East Coast counterpart. I had a hunch something was going on."

"That's sort of what we wanted to ask you about. Have you noticed a surge of paranormal criminal activity?"

She titled her head. "How do you mean?"

"A lot of weird shit happening."

The question made her a little agitated, but she was trying her best to conceal it from us. She wrapped herself in her arms and sat down. She looked like a woman that tried to put up a good front, but had just surrendered. She looked scared.

Mo'Lock pushed me towards her. I slapped him away, but gave in and moved around the couch. It took me a minute, but I eventually sat down awkwardly on the edge of the cushion. I looked over at her. Her face was different. Suddenly she was tired, worn out, and vulnerable. Her eyes were round and sad. I hated myself for thinking it, but she really looked beautiful. My heart beat faster and a wound on my lower back throbbed.

"You feel like talking?" I said.

She looked at me and for an instant I thought she was going to cry. "I'm sorry about running the story about you being a fraud. I trusted the contributor. I should have checked the sources."

"Water under the bridge, Lynch. That's not what's upsetting you."

She smiled faintly and let out a long, slow sigh. Then her face took on the strong, sharp-eyed look I'd seen before. "There have been a record number of sightings in the last month," she said. "Almost three times as many as I usually field."

Mo'Lock asked my question for me. "What do mean by sightings?"

"I get calls all the time. Most of the time they're cranks or crazies. I check most of them out on the off chance I'll get a story out of it, but it's usually a dead end."

"But lately?"

She tipped her head and blinked. "Lately it's been weird. I get a call about a ghost and I find evidence of a ghost. Last week, somebody reported a pride of werewolves killed downtown. I checked it out. Evidence points to werewolves, but they were all dead and I haven't figured out what happened."

I glanced at Mo'Lock.

"It's been this way every day," she went on. "Vampire reports, things flying in the sky over Griffith Park, people walking through walls, the dead coming back and contacting their loved ones…"

"Devil cult in Sherman Oaks?"

"Yeah. It's unbelievable. My whole career I've struggled to find enough material for four issues a year. Now, overnight, I'm getting enough leads to fill volumes!"

I shifted on the couch and our knees accidentally touched. "So something is going on. That's obvious. It's got to be either a random natural eruption of the supernatural or something that was caused by someone intentionally."

"As I've said, and it's been echoed by others, there appears to be a shift between the unnatural and natural world," Mo'Lock added. "What this means, I do not know. I can only say that my brethren are frightened, both on the East Coast and here in Los Angeles."

Lynch looked down and that frightened look returned. "Last night something happened that I can't explain," she said. There was an unsettling quiver in her voice. She stood and walked to the single large window in her small apartment.

"Around three o'clock last night I heard a scratching at the door. It was light, and I didn't get up until the sounds changed to a tapping. When I looked through the peephole, there was nothing there. I peeked through the shades…"

She looked white as a sheet. I followed her to the windows as she retraced her steps.

"There were two… people. Kids, I guess. Teenagers, standing out on the walkway staring at me."

"What'd they look like?"

"Dead. They looked *dead*. One of them, the tall one, his face was… gone; wiped away right down to the skull. The other kid, his skin was blue, and he was wet with black grease from his chest down."

She looked at me as if to see if I believed her. I did. She was probably talking to the one human being who would. Well, two, if you counted a decapitated head bouncing around the back of a truck in a box.

"Did they say or do anything?"

"No, they just stood there for hours, staring. It was horrible."

Although I had a pretty good idea who the kids were, now wasn't the time to fill her in. Why scare her more? They had to be Brian Hogue and Carl Potter, former playmates of Billy Fuller. Were the dead kids looking for help from Lynch because of her association with the occult? Or had Billy sent them as a warning to stop snooping around?

I was tempted to pay Billy a visit, but didn't dare as long as Sam's head was AWOL. With the head in postal limbo, the kid had the edge on us. We didn't want him to do something to permanently divide Sam from his torso. I'd have to wait and steer clear of Sherman Oaks for the time being.

I told Lynch not to worry, but to set up a camera to get pictures if the dead kids came back. She said she'd already planned on doing just that. I told her to call me if she was scared. That seemed to strike her as odd for some reason.

"Are you going to protect me?"

I felt myself starting to blush. "All I meant, Lynch, was... we're here if you need anything."

She batted her eyes at me. It was an act; I could see that. But it was working. Suddenly, I was having trouble breathing and wanted to get out of there fast.

"Please, call me Sabrina."

I didn't get a chance to reply. She duped me by turning her attention to Mo'Lock and left me standing there with red cheeks and a stupid look on my face.

She shook Mo'Lock's hand. "It was very good to meet you."

"The pleasure was mine, Ma'am." The ghoul bowed his head like some pansy from an old movie.

But Sabrina Lynch wasn't finished. She was angling for something. "Do you mind my asking exactly what you are?"

Mo'Lock touched his hand to his chest. "I'm undead. I am what humans call a ghoul."

"But I thought ghouls robbed graves and ate children."

Mo'Lock let out a stale breath. "I gave up eating children decades ago." He said with a twist of undead sarcasm. "However, certain factions of ghoul in the Midwest and Deep South still practice the eating of flesh."

"Would it be possible for me to get a photograph of you?"

Mo'Lock shook his head. "I'd rather not."

Sabrina was just about out of charm.

"Well, you still have the interview with me," I smirked.

Mo'Lock thanked Sabrina Lynch for her hospitality and walked out. I followed, giving her a wink on the way out. When she smiled, I could see it wasn't part of any act.

I followed Mo'Lock down the stairs to the pool where the hunchback had given up trying to snag the bottle. He sat with his feet in the water, eyeing the bobbing bottle like it was the greatest mystery of the 21st century.

We'd made it all the way back to the mailboxes when I turned and saw Sabrina outside her apartment, taking pictures of us. Mo'Lock and I flipped her off as we disappeared out of the steel gate. Let's see her print that.

1 8

There wasn't a hell of a lot

we could do to be proactive and that really had
me hot and bothered. I had to wait for Sam's head
to be re-redelivered so I could go after devil-kid
Billy. I also had to see what this fucking "day of
the monsters" shit would turn into, if anything.
These types of unnatural events are like a
hurricane. All you can do is sandbag the house.
It'll happen when it happens and you won't know
how bad it is until it's blowing seawater up
your nose.

   Mo'Lock was trying to convince me to get my
injuries checked out, but I wasn't having it.
Unless I was laid out on a stretcher, I had no
intention of going to a hospital. Besides, I had all
the prescriptions I needed. Instead, we wound

up cruising up Ventura Boulevard, near Sherman Oaks. I still didn't feel ready to corner Billy, but I thought we might as well stop in and see Sam's sheriff buddy, Ted Dawson.

Dawson's office was in a small municipal building on a side street, about four blocks from a mega-mall named after the area. As soon as we walked up to the main entrance I knew there was trouble. The flag on the roof was at half-mast. Somebody was dead and I had a gut feeling it was Dawson.

Inside, my hunch was confirmed without even talking to anybody. There were flowers all over the lobby and in the middle of the cluster was a photo of Sheriff Ted Dawson. Behind that was a huge sheet of paper signed by co-workers and locals with condolences.

Mo'Lock and I were about to leave—I knew Billy Fuller had something to do with the cop's death, and I didn't need specifics—when a deputy with a black arm band stepped up.

"Can I help you gentlemen with something?"

"Just came to pay our respects, "I said. "Dawson worked with a friend of mine."

The deputy nodded. "Shame, a man dying like that."

"Terrible." Suddenly I was curious and the deputy was in the mood to talk. "I mean, how could a guy die of a fall in the middle of nowhere?"

"Fall?"

"Yeah, didn't you hear? They found him in the middle of a high school football field in Burbank."

"Burbank? That's pretty far away."

"Yup. He'd died from a fall. Coroner said at least five, maybe as much as eight hundred feet in the air, except there ain't no building that high within a mile of the field! Explain that one." He shook his head, looking despondent and confused at the same time.

"Weird."

"Big weird," he said, then dropped a flower in front of the picture and left. I nudged the ghoul and we did the same.

•   •   •

We hit the road again. It was getting dark, so I steered us back towards Sam's. With any luck the package would be delivered in the morning. Then we could finally get on the case and nail this kid before he put a hex on the entire San Fernando Valley.

By the time we pulled onto Sam's street, it was pitch dark. Oddly, Benito and his half-baked vampire crew were nowhere to be seen. Since I'd arrived they'd always been on the streets or in one of the yards frying up some meat, playing music, and generally keeping an eye on the neighborhood. But this time, nothing. The ghoul and I were the only living (or non-living) souls on the street.

Then, as we prepared to head to the house, I noticed someone sitting in a car right across the street. I couldn't make out who it was because the entire cab was filled with smoke, like something out of a Cheech and Chong movie. I walked over and gave the window a tap. The window rolled down. Smoke rose from the crack and cleared the air enough so I could see Benito's pal, Junior, working on a joint the size of a polish sausage.

"What's up, Junior? Where's the gang?"

Junior was skinny as a rail and his shaved head and sunken red eyes gave him a mischievous look no matter what he said or did. "They got hungry."

Junior offered me the joint through the window. It had been a long time since I'd had any weed, so I took it and dragged off the stick hard. After about three hits I offered it to the ghoul. He shook his head, so I took two more hits and handed it back.

"Thanks."

"No sweat, monster man."

I smiled and walked away. As soon as the pot hit me I regretted taking it. My heart started pounding, and suddenly Mo'Lock freaked me out. He looked at me like a disappointed parent.

I scanned the dirt yard with its ugly rake marks, and suddenly the gash on my shoulder began to throb like a motherfucker. It hurt before, but this time it was different. It was a long, sustained ache that rose, fell, and was gone.

"What's wrong?"

"I dunno," I said, looking at the dirt and the deep raked grooves. "Something's not right here."

Mo'Lock stood alert and scanned around. He watched me as I stared at the yard and then upward to the sky. For some reason I thought of Dawson's eight hundred foot drop.

"What are you thinking?"

"I dunno," I repeated, but something was there. Something was right in front of me and I couldn't figure it out. Then again, maybe I was just stoned.

I decided I was being a tweak and headed into the house. As I stepped over the threshold every single cut, slash, gash, scrape, contusion, and bruise flared at the same time. I stumbled forward into the dark house, unable to ignore the pain. Mo'Lock grabbed hold of me, flipped the light and shut the door. At my feet I saw tiny pieces of shattered glass. It didn't take long for either of us to realize we were not alone.

Dave, the vampire I should have killed earlier, was waiting for me in Sam's living room.

He was to our right, standing next to the window he had obviously smashed through to get in. I'd thought he was ugly in the shadows of the Houdini house. In the dank yellow light of Sam's living room, he was absolutely fucking hideous. He had rough skin as white as boiled chicken meat, and this gross little upturned nose filled with ancient vampire nose-hair. Mo'Lock and I stood still and said nothing. It was a stand-off.

I couldn't take my eyes off his nose and I knew it was because I was high. He looked like a rabid pig in a suit. As soon as that thought entered my head, I laughed. The vampire was about to make his move, but my chuckle stopped him cold in his tracks, confused. It caught him completely off guard and gave Mo'Lock the opening he'd been waiting for.

The ghoul lunged at the bloodsucker and tackled him mid-torso. They hit the wall hard, shattering paint and plaster as they fell to the floor. The vampire hissed and kicked and clawed. Mo'Lock held his own, planting a rapid succession of alternating right and left hooks down on Dave's ugly-ass face.

It was dead versus dead. The Vampire kicked the ghoul off him. Mo'Lock landed on his feet. Dave did that vampire-rising-from-the-casket thing, rising straight to his feet, absolutely rigid, without bending a limb. Pretty impressive, actually.

I moved as far from the fight as I could and fell against the wall. My body was freezing up. Suddenly, I felt like I was dying. Either that or a major anxiety attack. The wounds all over my body were throbbing and stinging. Infection, I thought, it had to be infection. Please let it be an infection. I began to sweat profusely.

I turned around, still leaning on the wall, refusing to fall, until my back was resting against the surface. Mo'Lock and the vampire were really going at it, exchanging blows at speeds that blurred their motions. In a flash, the tide of battle had shifted and the ghoul was getting the worst of it. He was staggering back a bit and taking far more shots than he was throwing. Part of the reason was that the stupid ghoul kept looking over at me wriggling against the wall, sweating like some kind of freak.

In an instant, the vampire took total control of the brawl. He grabbed the ghoul by the throat and flipped him upside-down in a single move, slamming him head-first onto the floor. The wood slats cracked and Mo'Lock's head split open wide. The ghoul's thick, congealed blood spattered. Dave grabbed the dizzy ghoul's ankles and held him dangling off the ground. Now the vampire had a weapon. He was going to bludgeon me with my own partner.

I could barely move. The pain from the werewolf gashes and bites had spread like a fire burning beneath the surface of my skin. My muscles were so tight I could hardly manipulate my own limbs. All I could do was lean there against the wall and watch the ugliest bloodsucker in the world drag Mo'Lock towards me.

He started swinging Mo' around, at first in a circle, smashing two lamps and a half-full bottle of Vodka, then back and forth, *right* at me.

"Cal, get out of here! Run!" the vampire's baseball bat yelled out.

I leaned there helpless as Dave came at me, swinging Mo'Lock back and forth. I closed my eyes, more from the pain in my body than to brace myself for the blow.

Shit, how much more could it hurt after all I'd been through?

BAM!

Very, very much.

The first blow slammed me to the ground. The second missed, but took a chunk out of the wall above my head. Poor fucking Mo'Lock, getting smashed around like that. I knew he couldn't be killed, but shit, it had to be pretty fucking unpleasant.

I was on the ground trying to crawl away. BAM! Another narrow miss above my head. The vampire was laughing, the ghoul screaming and I was on the floor in a knot of pain. It was complete and total chaos. I scrambled weakly to my feet, and turned in time to see Mo'Lock's yowling face coming at mine and— BAM!—I was down. Mo'Lock was out cold. Even a ghoul has limits.

The vampire was laughing. My smashed face was running with blood. My body heaved. My body burned... and then it happened.

Clothes tore, muscles rippled and rolled. My eyes shot open, and even through the wash of blood over my face, I caught the vampire's expression as he dropped Mo'Lock and backed away.

He was scared.

I was changing.

I knew instantly what it was and it sure as fuck wasn't any infection. I was turning into a goddamn werewolf! The pain was gone and now most of my clothes were too. I watched the hair grow from my hands and up my arms, sprouting through the pores of my skin on every inch of my body. My bones snapped and reshaped like a dislocated joint popping back into place, and I felt a great strength and hunger growing inside me.

But best of all was watching the vampire shit his pants. That's right, you heard me. Shit ran right down his pant leg and plopped right onto the office floor!

I lowered my head, stood on my haunches and flexed my new, powerful lycanthrope body. My mind was intact. I was me. It was amazing. I was a werewolf!

So many thoughts shot through my head at once; most my own, but some primal and animalistic. Hundreds of questions, like how I was still in my right mind? But one thought prevailed and rose above the rest: *Rip that fucking vampire to shreds.*

I closed in, up on my haunches. The vampire was panicked. He was moving back and forth, trying frantically to decide where to go and what to do next. But no matter the direction he chose, I'd be on him in a heartbeat, and he knew it. I could see myself rending his flesh, ripping that misshapen nose from his face.

I imagined myself tearing into him. I pictured myself eating... and then I froze. Where the hell had that idea come from? I wanted to eat him. The mere thought of it made me drool. That was not good.

My hesitation gave the vampire a desperately needed opportunity. He turned and lunged through the window he'd come in. I reacted instantly, instinctively. No fucking way was he escaping. I wanted blood. His blood.

I ran like never before. My new legs pumped along at speeds I could scarcely imagine moments before. I started on my hind legs, but as I chased him into the more populated area around Ventura Boulevard, I went down on all fours and really let loose with some animal speed. Yet somehow I couldn't bring myself to take Dave down. The chase was too good. The hunt. I didn't want it to end. The sight of his frantically fleeing form, his face turning in fear to see if I was still there was too much to resist. I wanted it to go on forever.

Unfortunately, we were attracting a lot of attention as we sped through the streets and sidewalks of Studio City, although I was hardly aware of it. People were jumping out of our way, screaming and running indoors. I glimpsed my speeding reflection in a store window and saw just how frightening I looked.

I was huge, bigger than any wolf or dog could possibly be, and muscular like a man with animal-jointed limbs and a thick coat of black and gray hair. My eyes were piercing and alive, gleaming through my dark, furred face and extended snout. I was the perfect blend of animal and human. All these years hunting monsters and here I was a monster myself—and loving it!

The chase went on for a good mile and I didn't lose pace with him once. I blocked out the chaos around me and focused my acute senses. There was nothing I couldn't see, nothing I couldn't sniff out. Without looking, I knew that we had covered one mile, passed two hundred and twenty-three pedestrians and another three hundred and twelve people inside their cars. I felt their fear as they saw me, and their relief as I passed. I smelled their blood and wanted to taste it. At that moment, I knew that my current lucidity wasn't going to last. Eventually the bloodlust would take over and the human in me would disappear. It was a suddenly sobering thought in a moment when I felt the best I'd ever felt.

Fuck it. I couldn't do anything about it tonight. I might as well have fun and rid the world of one more bloodsucker.

I ran on, tireless. My nose focused on Dave and I sensed his fear of me suddenly subside. Something was wrong. He was leading me now. We were leaving Studio City and heading straight towards the LA River. I almost slowed down, knowing I was almost certainly running into a trap. But I was too far gone to be scared as my bloodlust welled to a breaking point. Trap or no trap, I was going to shred that vampire into tiny little bits and pull each and every nose hair from that ugly pug-nose.

We ran into a park as close as a foot apart. I could almost reach out and poke him with a claw. I smelled the trap, picturing it in my mind before I actually saw it.

We were running downhill, towards the huge, cement aqueduct that snaked throughout Los Angeles. Dave leaped a wire-mesh fence; I tore through it. Ahead was a clearing. At the bottom, the vampire took a sharp left, then swung around and faced me as I came to a halt. I could smell a presence around us. We were surrounded, but I was too focused on Dave to figure out how many or exactly where they were.

I sniffed the air and caught a whiff from the trees. The sound of water echoed through the cement channel. We stood facing each other in the pitch-black darkness of the park.

"Well?" I barked. "Your move, pig-face." My voice was gruff and phlegmy. My half-animal throat wasn't built for speech.

The vampire lunged. I stood my ground and cut him short, slashing his throat open with a swipe of my left while slashing his chest with my right. He reeled sideways and I slashed again, catching his shoulder. He was hemorrhaging stolen blood. Whatever he thought was going to happen, didn't.

I could smell panic rising in him again. Realizing his plan wasn't working, he began to back away. I advanced, snarling. He stumbled away, holding his throat as blood spewed through clamped fingers.

Behind the vampire's back, the cement river with its fetid water was close, and Dave knew it. He began scanning the tree tops. He wanted me to look, but I wasn't having it. I was locked on him as I rocked side to side, pacing in place, waiting for the moment that I would tear him into an unrecoverable pile of fleshy undead pieces.

I stepped forward and growled.

"Where are you?!" Dave cried out, and the trees began to rustle.

My radar-like senses went haywire. Suddenly, there were a hundred objects coming at me from every direction. I couldn't focus or get an exact fix on who or what I was smelling. I had seconds to act. I jumped forward and pounded the vampire with all my werewolf strength, which was evidently considerable. He flew through the air, flipping, turning, and screaming like a discarded doll, and landed head first in the running water inside the cement aqueduct.

It was a gamble. Running water affected only the most superstitious vampires. But considering Dave's age and his reaction to the makeshift cross, I hoped for the best. I hit pay dirt. He began to sizzle and steam like the Wicked Witch of the West, but I had barely a second to enjoy it before the screaming creatures from the trees finally found their target.

They were on me at once, hundreds of them, none bigger than a small cat. They frantically clawed and scratched me, pulling my hair and biting with sharp, needle-sized teeth. I slashed and pulled them off the best I could. They were like small gibbons, but bald and pink, with teeth so large I couldn't see how they fit into their tiny mouths. Their eyes were black, completely absent of pupils. And they were mean as fuck. They wouldn't stop. I ripped and slashed them to pieces, twisting their necks and killing them one by one, but there were too damn many of them. No matter how many I killed, there were ten to take its place.

Meanwhile, in two feet of moving water, Dave was dying slowly as he screamed for his creatures to kill me.

"Avenge me, my pets! Kill him!"

On the verge of death after hundreds of years, he still had time to be a melodramatic pansy. Incredible.

I wasn't doing much better. I was bleeding and taking heavy damage. They focused on wounds they'd made, tearing deeper and deeper into the tender flesh. I howled, spun and slashed, but I was losing.

I fell to the ground reeling and shook like a wet dog. They clung hard to the wounds, refusing to let go. The pain was so incredible, at first I didn't even realize I was suddenly hearing the creatures themselves shrieking in agony. Something was hurting them, something other then me. But it was too late. I collapsed on my side from loss of blood. I thought I was a goner for sure when I felt someone beside me, ripping the little monkey-vampires off.

When I finally looked up, I was surrounded again, but this time by friendly faces.

The first face
I saw was Junior.

Gradually, more came into focus; Benito Cruz and other neighborhood half-vampires, Mo'Lock and a gang of ghouls including Emek. They all stood there staring at the injured freak I was. Luckily, due to all the excitement, I was no longer high.

Benito stepped up and helped me to my feet.

"Man, you look fucked up, dude!"

I said thanks, but it came out more like "franks". The wolf throat didn't want to cooperate and I wished I was human again. As soon as the thought entered my brain, I felt my body begin to transform. With a crowd of gang-banging, semi-turned vampires and a few dozen LA ghouls watching, I went from total dog-boy to an upright half-man/half-wolf with a snout and fur-covered body. My clothes were completely gone, but my holster and gun had managed to hang on.

One of Benito's boys named Julio started laughing. "Dude, I think you looked better before!"

Everybody yucked it up at my expense until Mo'Lock came to my side and looked at me with an unreadable expression. The crowd milled around the grassy park. Nobody moved. The excitement was over. I didn't understand what the assembly was about. Something was up, and I has a sinking feeling I was the main attraction.

Mo'Lock stood over my wounded, furry body and took me by the shoulders. "Cal, how are you? How do you feel?"

"I feel like a guy who just turned into a fucking werewolf," I said, not altogether thrilled with the prospect of what I saw developing around me. The ghouls and vampires were watching me closely and I didn't like it. They were looking for something.

"A floodgate has been opened, Cal. We're all sure of it—we can all feel it." Mo'Lock gestured to his compatriots.

"So, what's that got to do with me?" I pushed him off me.

"You're part of it now, Cal. You're one of us."

"The fuck I am," I said.

I broke away from the group, feeling their eyes following me as I walked to the edge of the water to wash my wounds and drink. I had to resist the urge to lick myself, which only pissed me off more. At the stream's edge I got down on all fours and sniffed the water, then lapped up a few tonguefuls.

"There is a rash of unnatural incidents occurring all over the city. Emek was correct. Something big is happening." Mo'Lock came up behind me. "Cal, the city needs you."

I craned my head around. "Who're you, Jimmy Olson?"

I went back to drinking like a dog. The taste of the water was foul, dead, like there was more in it than just the rot of the city.

I should've seen it coming. Of course he wasn't dead. That would be too easy. I leapt up on my haunches, but it was too late. Dave came flying at me from the water, wailing like a freaking banshee.

He was almost completely skinned. His flesh had melted from the bone. I didn't want him to touch me and fell backwards against Mo'Lock, who was no less repulsed than I. The crowd of ghouls and vampire bangers screamed and scattered around us. I rolled, avoiding the bloody bone-hands that reached for me. Mo'Lock wasn't so lucky. As I jumped up, I saw the vampire lift the ghoul off the ground and toss him away like a rag-doll. Mo'Lock hit a tree and slid to the ground headfirst.

That was it. I was pissed off.

I moved towards Dave. He was little more than a dripping skeleton. He had only one eye in his skull, which he was using to scan the ground where the shredded bodies of his monkey-things lay scattered. He backed away, but there wasn't going to be any goddamn chase this time. I moved fast, and slammed my fist straight into the side of his skull. It exploded like a tomato in a microwave, glorious fireworks of bone and blood.

The headless vampire stood in place, swaying for a moment, then collapsed in a heap of bones and slime. It was over.

The half-vampires and ghouls began to come up to me. One started clapping, then another. Soon the entire crowd was applauding, including Mo'Lock. It really got to me, so I reared back my head and howled at the sky.

Then I stopped. What the fuck was I doing? I couldn't live like this—the very thing I'd made a living hunting and destroying.

I gestured for everybody to shut the hell up, and turned to Benito and Mo'Lock. They were waiting for some kind of answer from me. First I had to take care of business.

"If something is happening, I'll be your personal bloodhound. Everybody keep their ears to the ground. If there's been a sudden surge in paranormal activity, there has to be a reason and a source, so let's wait and see what happens, okay?"

The crowd all nodded to each other. Benito turned and gave a signal to his boys and they began to head out.

"Right now all I want is a thousand beers and some sleep."

Mo'Lock and I walked the other way as the crowd dispersed. I turned full-wolf and dropped to all fours without even realizing it. I felt a terrible sense of dread and loss, a sadness I'd never felt before. I should have been exhilarated with all this power, but I wasn't. It felt as uncomfortable as an itchy sweater. The werewolf thing was cool, but it wasn't me.

For now, I knew I could somewhat control my transformations between human and lycanthrope, but what would happen when the bloodlust took over? I could lose control. I couldn't live with that.

"Will I ever be a real human again?" It came out sounding a little more desperate then I'd intended.

"I'm not sure," said the ghoul. "Have you ever heard of a cure for shape-shifters?"

"No. But if there is, I'm going to find it. I have no intention of spending my life resisting the urge to eat everybody I meet."

"And I don't want to have to take you for walks."

"Fuck off."

chapter

2 0

Back at Sam's place, a miracle

occurred. The Red Sea parted, one loaf of bread became a thousand, the sky rained frogs, and in the year 2003, the United States Postal Service actually managed to deliver a package.

Mo'Lock and I had been back for less then an hour. I'd shifted back to human form and showered. All my original wounds were healed, now replaced by injuries made by little monkey-vamp bites. I couldn't catch a break. I was doomed to be covered with stinging, painful wounds for the rest of my life.

Mo'Lock and I came as close as we ever do to arguing about the whole floodgate thing he and Emek had been going on about. I had my ideas and they were nowhere near as sinister as his. While the ghouls thought there was some kind of monster apocalypse coming, I thought there was single cause for all of this. I didn't want to say anything until I was sure, though.

That's what triggered the fight.

Mo'Lock hated that I didn't share my every thought with him. Fuck him. This wasn't the Oprah Show. This was my fucking life. I'd talk when I wanted to talk.

Finally, he got pissed off and stormed to the door. He almost tripped over the large, battered box on the step. Mo'Lock forgot he was mad and picked up the parcel.

There was no movement or sound coming from the battered carton. I feared the worst and immediately tore at the tape.

The top layer was all crumpled paper and little Styrofoam peanuts. I pulled the paper away, sending peanuts flying. For half a second I thought the box was empty.

"IT'S ABOUT TIME YOU FOUND ME, YOU STUPID MOTHER-FUCKER!" blared from the box, accompanied by the foul stench of an unbrushed mouthful of nasty old teeth.

The ghoul and I had to back away. It was *that* bad. I tried to get Mo' to pull the screaming head out, but he pushed me forward. I held my breath and reached into the box. Inside I felt the hot, sweaty, semi-haired, completely scarred head of my old buddy Sam Burnett and lifted it to freedom. Half-melted packing peanuts peppered his face, and Styrofoam fragments were all over his mouth. He'd been eating the packing peanuts to survive. I would have laughed, but that was some fucked up shit.

As I rested the head onto the coffee table I shot the ghoul a look. "Mo'Lock. Listerine. Bathroom. Now!"

Sam was ranting, screaming, and throwing insults at a machine gun pace as I made a comfortable resting place for him on the table. The words I could take, but the breath? Damn! Finally Mo'Lock came running back with the bottle of mouthwash. I grabbed it and poured it into Sam's mouth. He resisted at first, but finally gargled.

I felt like I'd deactivated a nuclear missile.

"So you fuckheads destroyed my house yet?"

I smiled. "Oh, and thank you for traveling cross-country to help my sorry old ass, and…"

"All right, all right!" Sam yelled. "Fill me in. Where's my body? You deal with Billy yet?"

I fish-eyed the ghoul. "No. We've been waiting for you."

Sam flipped out. Well, as much as a solo head can flip out. "What?! You mean to tell me you've been out here for a week plus and you've done nothing about finding my body?! What the fuck have you been doing?!"

"Been pretty busy, actually."

"Shut up!"

He was one angry head, but he didn't know the details. I filled him in on the flurry of activity, from the hipster werewolves to the showdown with Dave. I ended by updating him on the fate of his sheriff buddy. Sam took it pretty well. He screamed and yelled and somehow managed to turn his face red as a ripe tomato.

"How could he have fallen from that high in the middle of nowhere?" he asked when he had finally calmed down. "Any reports of flying beasties?"

"I don't know, Sam," I said. "Give me a chance to think. There's a pattern here somewhere, I can feel it. I'm pretty sure that Billy is a key element."

"You think so, shithead?"

I turned and pointed right in Sam's face on the coffee table. "You better start showing a little respect, or so fucking help me, I'll punt you all the way back to DC."

Sam smiled. "There you go. That's more like it."

When I turned, Mo'Lock was glaring at me. "You talk to him. Couldn't you have told me?"

I started to tell him to fuck off, but he was right. I nodded and gave his shoulder a little slug. "No reason at all. Sorry."

I looked in my pockets for anything to give me a buzz but came up empty. Things were getting fucked up fast. I started getting cravings. Now, on top of it all, I was a part-time werewolf. I could feel their eyes on me, but I ignored them and lit a cigarette. I dug through my desk and found the last of the stash of Meth that I kept taped under the top drawer. It had survived the move.

I put the little glass bottle up to one nostril, held the other closed and snorted the crystals into my head. It stung, but within seconds I felt the effects. I chased it with a drink. Now I was ready for work.

Mo'Lock was frozen at the front window. I watched him until one of his eyebrows rose. He turned his head toward me and pointed with his thumb. "Cops are here."

I looked up, and sure as shit there were two LAPD blues getting out of a squad car in front of the house.

"Goddammitmotherfuckingshit," I muttered. I wiped my nose with the back of my hand. "Cover the head!"

Mo'Lock grabbed a dish rag and started to cover Sam's head until Sam spoke up. "Mojo, Moby… whatever the fuck yer name is," he yelled, "don't cover me. Look at the cops again."

Mo'Lock looked out the window once more as the two blues walked slowly up the sidewalk. I watched a slow, almost sinister grin grow across his lips, and I knew what Sam wanted him to see. They were ghouls. LAPD ghouls.

One was clean-cut, tall, and blonde with a short crew-cut. His badge read Hamm. The other was African-American, clean-cut, with light eyes and a shaved head. His badge read Shooter. The blonde looked from me to Mo'Lock to the head on the table and nodded.

"Sam Burnett. We need to talk to you."

The head on the table was happy as hell to be the center of attention. "Good to see you boys. What's the rumpus?"

The ghoul cops looked at each other, confused. I stepped up and introduced myself and Mo'Lock and took over the conversation. "What's the trouble, officer?"

Shooter looked at me. His eyes were bright and dead at the same time, with a cold stare that gave me chills. My guess was that this is what you got when you combined the laid-back ease of a ghoul and the manic reality of a cop. What I couldn't guess was if it was a good thing. I was used to the East Coast type of ghoul.

"The Griffith Park Observatory," Shooter said, speaking like a machine. "There's some sort of disturbance up there. We have significant undead numbers on the force and we've managed to keep most of this below the radar of the humans. But if something isn't done soon, the results could be devastating."

I gestured for more. "What sort of disturbance?"

Hamm pulled out a Polaroid and flipped it to me. I caught it and looked at the snap as Mo'Lock peered over my shoulder. It was a shot of the observatory. I'd seen it before in films and TV, but now it looked different. The building was completely covered with scaffolding, but I'd heard it was shut down for renovation. No mystery there.

But the something else had no easy explanation: There was a black tear floating in mid-air, just above the yard of the historic building. A black, floating hole and something was crawling out of it.

Before I could ask what it was, Hamm handed me another photo that showed what the hell that "something" was. It was red, with bat-like wings, horns all over its body, and the burning eyes of a demon. I didn't think I was going out on a limb guessing the floating tear was some sort of portal.

In the second picture, the red demon was airborne just outside the rip. It didn't take long for me to put two and two together, but Mo'Lock beat me to the punch.

"This would explain what happened to Sheriff Dawson."

"Let me see!" Sam screamed from the table.

Mo'Lock lifted Sam's head and hoisted him for a look, but something caught his eye before he saw the photos.

"Wait!"

Mo'Lock stopped at the open front door where Sam was looking outside at the dirt covered yard.

"What's up?" I asked.

"Not much," he said, "but last time I was home I had a fucking lawn."

* * *

We were all outside looking at the raked dirt surrounding Sam's house, but beside the inarguable fact that someone had stolen Sam's lawn, there wasn't a lot to see. I recalled my earlier thoughts of Dawson. With the flying demon added to the mix, I had an angle.

"Sam, you have a ladder?"

"Yeah, it's in the gardening shed with my other supplies," Sam spat. "No, you stupid fuck, I don't!"

I ignored the sarcastic head and asked Shooter to give me a leg up to the porch overhang. From there I could get to the roof. I had a hard time climbing at first, until I remembered the little bug I'd picked up. I concentrated hard, seeing if I could transform only a little. I didn't want to become a full werewolf and ruin another set of clothes, but I needed the added strength and agility. It worked. My body stayed the same, but my teeth and snout turned slightly doggish. Thank God nobody could see me.

Once on the roof, I looked down at the dirt and my hunch bore fruit. There were markings in the dirt, strange lines and squiggles going all the way around and forming a circle. Suddenly my current run of bad luck began to make sense.

"Hey Sam, what did the kid used to trap you?" I yelled down.

Sam paused. "I told you... a magic circle."

"Well, one guess what's surrounding your house."

2 1

We destroyed the circle. Hamm and

Shooter worked side by side with Mo'Lock and
me as we kicked and spread the dirt, destroying
every last symbol etched into the earth. Sam
rested on the porch by the door.

When we finished the yard, I started giving
orders. I told Mo'Lock to go to the observatory
with the LAPD ghouls and see what could be
done about the tear in the air. "At the very least
try to capture or kill whatever comes out of
there."

"We've been trying," Shooter said.

"Try harder."

Mo'Lock stepped up. "What about you?"

"The head and I are going to pay a visit to
Billy's house."

"What if he isn't the cause of all this?" the ghoul asked.

"I can smell his stinky teenage sweat all over this dirt. It's him all right, and I'll lay money that he's behind the tear. Looks like devil boy isn't just happy messing with this dimension. Now he's breaking into others."

"He might destroy Sam's body if you get too close."

I smiled. "At this point, that's a gamble I'm willing to take."

From the porch Sam yelled, "Hey, fuck you!"

"Besides," I went on as I grinned, "I don't think Billy's ready for what I've become."

Mo'Lock nodded. "Human magic versus monster magic."

"Two different applications." I smiled wide and showed my new canines.

If I concentrated, I could make them shoot in and out of their sockets. I might have been fucked up, but I had this werewolf thing by the balls.

* * *

Mo'Lock and the undead cops left for Griffith Park, so I picked Sam's head up and headed into the house for some supplies.

Once again I needed to suit up for a fight with an enemy that had the upper hand. I hated that. But I had a few things on my side, not the least of which was how pissed I was that the little fucker had put a curse on the house and almost got me killed no less then three times. I was gonna bitch-slap that prick like he'd never been bitch-slapped.

Inside I loaded up the .38 and packed a spare. Unfortunately, with this type of scenario there wasn't really much specialized equipment. Holy water, silver bullets, and all that were only for certain sects within the monster community. I did take a small anti-magic amulet with me, just in case, but I prefer not to rely on things like that. As far as I'm concerned, it's like using the enemy's weapons.

Besides, we were dealing with something very different; the human monster. All I could really bring to the party was some heat and my brains. Oh, and my leather sap, in case the whole thing could be solved by a crack to the skull.

I put Sam in a box with a towel and prepared to head out, but as I lowered him into the box, an ominous and familiar click came from the open front door. I was frozen, holding the head and staring dumbly as Sabrina lowered her camera and grinned like a fiend.

"Monster hunter kills competition," she said. "I can see the headline now."

Then Sam opened his eyes and yelled, "Can't you see we're busy!"

Sabrina almost dropped her camera. She staggered into the house and then back against the wall for support. I prayed she'd faint so we could make a break, but she was too tough. She gathered her composure with a few deep breaths. Within fifteen seconds she was cool, calm, and ready for another shock. That tore it—I liked her.

"We have some metalhead in Sherman Oaks that's been playing with satanic rites and interdimensional tampering. Possibly conjuring curses—the whole gamut of nasty evil," I said, lowering Sam into the box once more. "Sounds like the kid started out playing, but we have a trail of bodies…"

"Brian Hogue, Carl Potter and Sheriff Dawson," Sabrina said as she came up to me. "They were the apparitions outside my window."

I shot her a quick glance. "Dawson too?"

"Wha? Who? Dawson?! I thought he was dead!" Sam was freaking out in the box.

I waved for Sam to shut up.

I grinned. "So, they appeared again?"

She grinned back. "This time I went outside and confronted them. They wanted my help."

"Could this get any fucking weirder?" Sam yelled from the box.

"They talked to you?" I added.

She stepped closer to me. "That's all they wanted. They'd gained some power working with Billy, learning Satanic rites. They used the last of their power to contact me and tell me how they were killed."

"By curses Billy Fuller put on them?"

She nodded slowly. "Yeah. Sounds like they were all buddies. They experimented with the whole witchcraft, devil thing… then Billy screwed them. Hogue and Potter were just into it for kicks. Fuller got serious." She was staring at me as she talked.

I swallowed hard. Suddenly, it was getting hot. Something about her confronting the apparitions, I don't know, turned me on.

"Why was Dawson with them?"

"Some spirit world unity. Victims bound together, united in exposing their killer." She was whispering.

"Oh," was all I could muster.

We had both moved forward. We were close, inches apart. My whole body was about to start shaking, so I just did it. I leaned in and kissed her and, thank God, she did the same. It had been a long time since I'd kissed a woman, but it never felt like this. Kissing Sabrina felt right.

After a long pause, we parted. We both smiled and laughed, shy like kids. It was the perfect moment, a moment about to be shattered by a pissed off head.

"This is all very touching, but in case you haven't noticed… I DON'T HAVE A MOTHERFUCKING BODY AND I SURE WOULD LIKE TO GET THIS GODDAMN SHOW ON THE ROAD!"

I closed the box. Billy could wait another hour.

2 2

Sabrina wanted to come with Sam

and me to Billy's place in Sherman Oaks, but I didn't like the idea. The kid was way too dangerous. Luckily when I told her about the rip and the demon that had been spotted coming out, she decided the observatory had better photo opportunities.

I watched her walk to her Beetle and glance back at me no less than three times with a stupid grin plastered on my face that was impossible to erase. I hardly even noticed Sam yelling from inside the box as I carried him to my car, but once we started driving he was hard to ignore. He didn't shut up the entire trip. He bitched about how I treated him, he bitched about being severed from his body, he even bitched about being hungry and having to piss.

That's when I pulled the car over.

"What do you mean you have to piss?"

"I gotta piss and I'm hungry."

"You felt this before?"

"Not like this," said the head in the box.

I licked my lips. "Could mean we're close to where your body is being hidden."

"It could mean Billy is shoving corncobs up my ass," Sam blurted. "Let's move, asshole!"

I drove off the shoulder and took an extra sharp turn so Sam rattled inside the box like a melon. We drove straight to Billy's house, a small but nice place in a quiet, middle-class neighborhood. It was kind of on the sleepy side, but kind of on the snooty side, as well.

The Fuller house was a one story rancher with green shutters and matching trim. I parked a few doors away and left the head behind with the windows rolled down for air. I needed both of my hands to work. This was dangerous work, not fucking football.

There was only one car in the Fuller driveway, a run-down, older model sedan. In fact, of all the houses on the block, the Fuller's looked the worst. It was obvious there was trouble inside. Homes have a way of outwardly showing the distress of their occupants. Whether it's an unkempt lawn or a thick layer of pizza menus on the doorknob, I've found that people always have ways of crying out without actually making a sound.

I tapped lightly on the door. Nothing. I tapped again, then rang the bell. Within seconds I heard movement, a muffled female voice, and the door being unlocked from the inside.

A middle aged woman wearing a Denny's waitress outfit answered the door. She had a pretty face, but wore a tired, haggard expression. You didn't have to be a psychic to read this one: divorced, trying to survive on her own and keep the house by going back to work. Waitressing was the only thing she could find and it was killing her. Plus, she had Billy for a kid. I felt bad for her.

As soon as she saw me, she slumped and sighed.

"Oh dear, what's he done now?"

She thought I was a cop. I let her. "Maybe you can tell me, ma'am."

"Call me Doris," she said. "Come in. I was just making some Sanka."

It was a normal house in every way, but oddly dated. The living room was off to the right of the foyer. The entire color scheme was dull orange and brown. There was a TV, a couch, a lima bean-shaped coffee table and a painting depicting a snowy lake scene with a gold frame frosted with white. It screamed, *Better Homes and Garden* circa 1977. It reminded me of the house I grew up in. As soon as I saw the giant wooden fork and spoon hanging on the kitchen wall, I felt right at home. We sat down at a small, round, Formica-topped table while

Doris Fuller poured two cups of steaming hot instant joe. I couldn't take my eyes off the wallpaper. It was yellow with a velvet paisley pattern.

She smiled at me and lowered her eyes, as if waiting for more shit to be dumped on her head. I knew she had no idea of the evil being generated in her home. In fact, I was amazed I hadn't felt anything. Usually when I stepped into a threatening atmosphere, I could feel a strange tension in the air, or lately, in my wounds. Here I felt nothing. It was clean.

"Things have been terrible around here, what with all the deaths. Poor Billy has been so depressed," she sighed. "Frankly, I'm worried."

"Well, that's why I'm here, Doris," I said in my best soothing voice.

"I know, I know. It's about the Wayside Cemetery, isn't it? I caught him sneaking in late last night and he told me where he'd been. I gave him what for and he promised me he'd stay away from there once and for all." She ended with a sip and smile, leaving a red ring on the rim of the mug.

Wayside Cemetery.

That had to be where Sam's body was stashed.

I pretended to sip the hot swill. "Well, Doris, it sounds like you have things well in hand here. Is Billy home by any chance?"

She gave me the "go on" gesture. "Yes. The little bugger caught himself a devil of a cold last night. He's asleep upstairs, so if it isn't absolutely necessary, I'd prefer it if we just let him be."

"I guess there's no reason to bother him," I said, standing. "Just make sure he stays out of that cemetery, okay."

I smiled and gave her a wink. Big mistake.

She hurried after me and tried to block my way out. "I didn't catch your name, Mr...."

"McDonald, ma'am. Cal McDonald."

"Is there a Mrs. McDonald?"

I sidestepped her and tried to smile, but she had me cornered. "No, there isn't."

She smiled and poofed her hair net. "Maybe you could stop by again for something a little stronger than Sanka."

I bowed my head. "That would be nice, Doris," I offered weakly, ducking out of the house like a cat on fire. I had to wave back at her fifteen fucking times before she finally closed the door.

Back in the car, I updated Sam, and we waited half an hour for Doris to leave for Denny's. As soon as her car turned the corner and disappeared I went into action. I went to the back door of the house and jimmied the sliding glass door, then crept down a narrow hall until I saw a door with a "No Humans Allowed" sign.

I placed the anti-magic amulet around my neck. If the punk tried anything it would bounce right off me, but I still felt like a jackass wearing it. All I needed was some sandals and patchouli and I was ready for the smoke-in. I also had my newfound werewolf power as a back-up. Between the two I figured I could take the kid down and put an end to this bullshit once and for all.

I tried the doorknob and it gave, revealing every teenage reject's room rolled into one. Posters, mostly metal and industrial bands, covered the walls and ceiling. Trash littered the floor. There was a purple, plastic bong and beer bottles, and an ashtray full of butts and spent matches. The bed was a single mattress tucked between the TV and the stereo.

The mattress was stuffed with sheets and pillows to make it look like someone was sleeping in it. I intentionally stood there and stared at the bed, looking as dumb as I could. I even went a little slack-jawed, but what I was really doing was increasing the *wolfishness* of my ears and eyes just enough to read the room without looking around. Because, despite appearances, I wasn't alone.

There was a closet to my right. I could feel Billy eyeing me through the wooden slats.

I decided it was time he had a little scare of his own. I took out my backup piece, a .45 with a handy-dandy silencer, then stepped over to the bed and unloaded the entire clip into the pile under the blankets. I riddled the fake body until the room was filled with smoke and feathers.

After the last shot, a whimpering gasp came from the closet.

I turned and leveled the gun on the closet. "Get out here."

Billy Fuller came out. He was as skinny as a flagpole. His hair was long and greasy and acne covered his cheeks. He wore a Skid Row t-shirt. He was not only evil, but horribly behind the times.

Billy was shaking, but his eyes were darting side-to-side. I could see he still had a trick up his sleeve. Even so, I was shocked when he came at me, stopping within a foot, raising an amulet of his own, and chanting.

"Ammul Kanna Keela!"

I yawned and showed him the charm around my neck. "Sticks and stones, punk," I barked, slapping him so hard he flew against the wall. My hand had a thick coating of Clearasil across the palm. I walked over and lifted him up by his t-shirt.

"I'm gonna ask you this once, kid. If I don't get the answer I want, I'm gonna shove the gun up your ass and play butthole roulette. Where's the incantation you used on Sam Burnett?"

Billy peed himself. "I threw it away."

The pip-squeak still had some fight in him. He was so small. I had to remind myself that he was also a killer.

"Don't bullshit me, Billy," I said, pulling his face close to mine. "I know if you throw away the incantation, the curse won't work. I've been at this a lot longer than you, so don't bullshit a bullshitter."

I gave him a quick yank. Our noses touched, and for a single instant I allowed my face to shift to a wolf, then back again. I just wanted to give him a peek.

"Where's... the fucking... incantation?"

He was beaten. The kid pointed to the bong. I threw him onto the bullet-riddled mattress and turned the bong over. Taped to the base was a small piece of parchment with some mumbo-jumbo scrawled on it. I took the paper and turned to Billy as I reloaded my piece.

"The body. It's at Wayside Cemetery, right?"

Billy nodded.

"Where?" I slammed another clip into the .45.

He shook and started to cry. "There's a tomb for the dick who founded this piece-of-shit town. I left it in there."

"Good boy. Now listen to me," I said reholstering my heater, "You're gonna clean yourself up good, then you're gonna march yourself down to the sheriff's office and turn yourself in. You're a kid. You'll get the easy treatment and a lot of attention. You'll be the most popular psycho in the state."

The kid stared at me blankly.

I waved. "Hello? You understand? Otherwise, I come back with Sam in one piece. Believe me, that old son-of-a-bitch will tear you apart. He isn't as understanding as me."

Finally the kid nodded. I turned my back, knowing if the kid didn't try anything with my defenses down he'd do as I told him.

"*Satana Karise!*"

A bolt of pain shot through my body like electricity. I yelled and fell to one knee. The little fucker had no intention of letting up.

When I turned back, Billy wasn't alone. We had some company. A red, winged creature stood behind him, in front of a black portal ripped into the air. I stood back up and looked at the kid. He was smirking, his greasy hair slung down over one eye. My blood boiled. Who did this little punk-ass bitch think he was?

"Nice try, mister. But I have friends now—real friends—and they'll protect me against you and anybody else who tries to stop me. We made a deal."

I stared up at the demon, maybe the same one who'd dropped the sheriff to his death, and I could see by the look in its narrow eyes the kid was right. If I wanted Billy Fuller, I'd have to take on the creature first. I put my piece back in the holster and began to selectively transform myself. My hands changed to claws, my jaw sprouted wolf-teeth, and I increased my bulk just enough to not tear apart my clothes.

I was ready for a fight.

The creature took Billy by the shoulder and stepped around him. It rattled its wings and licked its long nails.

I waited.

It made the first move. It came at me shrieking and tackled me head on. I took the blow and fell backwards, but managed to rake my claws across its lower back. It yowled and rolled off me. As it turned back to attack, I slashed its throat wide open. The shrieking stopped. Blood sprayed.

The demon tried to struggle away, but I knew I had it down for the count. I lunged on top of it and brought it down hard. I tore at its wings, pulling one completely out of its back. Finally, the creature stopped moving.

Just to be sure I'd killed it (and to put a scare into the kid), I pulled out my piece and blasted a slug into the demon's head, blowing its supernatural brains all over the shag carpet.

Victorious, I stood and shook the blood from my body like a dog after a bath. But I'd miscalculated.

Billy Fuller was gone, and so was the rip in the air.

2 3

Before I left
the Fuller house

I covered the dead demon with a sheet and took
a hit off the kids bong. I knew I'd sort of freaked
the last time I got high, but it looked like the kid
had some pretty good stuff.

I told Sam what happened on the way to the
cemetery. Billy Fuller had more tricks up his
sleeve and we had to stop him before he realized
how much damage he could do. If he'd actually
made a deal with some sort of demonic power,
the repercussions could be catastrophic for both
the kid and Los Angeles.

Sam, of course, was an unstoppable ball-
breaker about the whole thing.

"Well, little Cal fucked up again. I woulda
killed the little fucker when I had the chance."

"Lay off. I ain't killing no little kid, no matter what he did," I said, driving through the cemetery gate.

"You are such a pussy. I don't know how you survive."

That was it. I slammed on the brakes and stopped the car. The box with Sam in it went flying to the floor.

I grabbed it and leaned in. "I just saved your ass, old man. Don't you think it's about time for a little respect?"

Sam's head rolled its eyes. "Sorry."

"And?"

"Thank you."

I nodded and grabbed the box. The tomb was right in the center of the otherwise plain graveyard. It had a big steel door, chained shut. The padlock was brand new, so I knew it was Billy's doing. I blasted the lock with the silencer and pushed the door open. Daylight flooded into the crypt.

Inside, on a white stone block, was Sam's headless body sitting like a guy waiting for the bus. It was slumped over, and the raggedy old suit it wore was covered with mud and dust. I took out Sam's head and placed it next to the body, and then made the first in a series of big mistakes.

I touched the body.

The damn thing flipped out. It went completely fucking nuts, swinging its arms and running around the tomb like a spastic child on fire. It was out of control, running in circles. I tried to grab it but it was too much to handle. Sam screamed. I screamed back. The headless body decided to bolt out of the tomb, making a blind run for it.

"Careful! Don't hurt my fucking body! Catch it!" Sam screamed.

"I'm trying! I'm trying!"

I chased the body all over the graveyard as it juked and hurdled headstones. How it knew where the obstacles were was anybody's guess. I finally got pissed and ran at the thing full speed. I tackled it, then held it in a bear hug and hauled it back to the tomb. Once inside, I pinned it securely next to it's head.

"Now burn the incantation!"

"I know what to do, Sam."

"Burn it!"

I lit the parchment. As it burned, Sam's head began to levitate as the lines of time and space sparked and smoked. By the time the small paper was ash, Sam and his body were reunited—all five foot four of his cranky ass.

"Man, I gotta piss like nobody's business!"

"Hold it. We gotta get up to Griffith Park and see what's happening up there."

"I ain't doing anything until I piss and get some food!"

Fine. We stopped at a burger joint on the way to the park. Sam drained himself and ate five hamburgers without taking a breath. After nearly choking to death, he was ready for action.

"Let's go kill this little bastard," Sam smiled. Every scar on his messed-up head moved like a thousand tiny grins.

I was about to pull away from the burger dump when suddenly everything went black. And I mean everything, including street lights and the sun. In the blink of an eye, total darkness—like an instant eclipse. Everything came to a halt and for one nanosecond, the world was silent. A beat later, I began hearing screams and car horns in the darkness. It was as black as a starless midnight sky. People were panicking.

A car, practically on two wheels, came smashing through the side of the restaurant wall and landed on top of a table of six with a thunderous, smoking crash. There was blood and smoke and screaming everywhere. I yelled for someone to call an ambulance.

As we moved through the unnatural dark, the entire city was in chaos. There were screams and crashes everywhere. In the sky I heard helicopters, but couldn't see them. People were running into the streets and getting struck down by cars. It was horrible.

Though we wanted to, we didn't allow ourselves to stop and help. I looked over at Sam as we drove towards the park. There was a horror in his eyes I'd never seen before. Maybe the ghouls had been right all along. The floodgates had opened. The day of the monsters was upon us, and it was all that little fucker Billy's fault.

Maybe, if we hurried, we could do something about it. If not, we were in for a long period of darkness, and most likely, the end of life as we knew it.

I drove through the darkness like a madman, from Sherman Oaks to North Hollywood, but just as I prepared to make the turn to the observatory, I saw a nightmare. Just ahead of us, a woman was being dragged from her car by a red, winged creature identical to the one I killed. I slammed on the brakes and came to a sudden stop, catching the woman and the creature in my headlights.

As I ran towards the action, the creature stopped, and tried to take flight. I lowered my .45 and aimed.

BLAMM! The shot tore through the side of the demon's face. It released the woman, who wisely ran away in a screaming panic. I shot again. This time I hit it square in the forehead. It dropped to the pavement like a big wet rag, but I didn't get two seconds to enjoy the victory. Sam tapped my shoulder and pointed up. The black sky filled with flying creatures.

"You have an extra piece?"

I handed him my.38 snub-nose.

"What are we gonna do?" I'd never heard that tone in Sam Burnett's voice. It was fear, plain and simple. Fear and helplessness.

"I don't have a clue."

But I knew whatever we could do had to start at that rip in the air. Somewhere in that black hole was the answer. As we got back to the car, three demons landed and stole away the body of their fallen comrade. Before they flew off again, they looked at me and hissed.

I reached for my gun, but Sam grabbed my arm. "Don't waste your time, son. Let's get to the observatory."

He was right. I peeled out of there, doing eighty down a residential street until I cut back onto Alameda. And then once on Victory, I opened her up to almost a hundred. Every time Sam looked up he saw creatures flying in all directions. Some of them had people in their claws.

I turned on the radio.

"...UNKNOWN SPECIES OF CREATURES NUMBERING IN THE HUNDREDS ARE ATTACKING AND KILLING CITIZENS. THERE IS NO WORD ON WHAT THEY ARE OR WHY THEY ARE ATTACKING...""

It was madness.

I changed the station.

"...CITIZENS ARE WARNED TO STAY IN THEIR HOMES..."

I turned off the radio. Christ.

Just as I saw the hills of Griffith Park ahead through the bleak haze of darkness, I noticed movement on the streets. Instead of listening to the radio reports, people were coming out of their homes and into the streets. Suddenly there was a crowd in front of me. I slammed on the brakes and skidded within an inch of killing more then a dozen people.

But they weren't people. It was Emek and a group of other ghouls. Emek came around to the window.

"What's the word?" I asked.

"Complete chaos."

"I'm heading up to the observatory. Can you and your buddies deal with the... whatever the fuck they are?"

Emek nodded.

"Thanks. Sam, head back to your place," I said as I began to shift to my wolf form, "I'll go the rest of the way on foot."

I was gone before he even answered.

2 4

I dropped on all fours and ran

into the park as fast as my legs would carry me. I could smell action ahead. The scent of Mo'Lock and Sabrina guided me to the top of the thickly wooded hill.

The observatory came into view at the crest of the hill. There was a small crowd waiting. Mo'Lock stood by Sabrina near the main building, speaking with the two LAPD ghouls. At the gate of the observatory grounds other cops guarded the roads. I assumed they were ghouls too, but it was the floating black hole that I was most interested in. That was my way to get to Billy and put an end to this madness once and for all.

Mo'Lock, Sabrina, and the cops approached me as I rose to my feet and shifted back to human. Sabrina was looking at me strangely, but I couldn't tell if she'd seen me in wolf form or not.

"Anything happened here? The valley is bedlam."

"A bunch of those red things flew out," Mo'Lock said, "but we couldn't do anything. It was right after it went dark."

Sabrina smiled. "I got the photos to prove it."

I smiled at her. If she saw me shift, she wasn't letting on.

Hamm and Shooter looked worried. "We have a report of another hole in South Central," Hamm said.

Shooter finished. "If this spreads much further, we won't be able to do anything to stop it."

I looked at the rip. "Mo'Lock, give me a leg up. I'm going in."

"I'm going with you," Mo'Lock insisted.

I pulled him aside and whispered. "Not this time, buddy. I think this Billy kid made some sort of deal with an evil force… a spiritual force. I don't think someone of your undead nature should be messing around in there."

Mo'Lock looked to see if anybody was listening. "Are you saying the hole is the gateway to…"

"I'm not saying anything for sure. But if it is, you could put yourself in danger, not having a soul and all."

The ghoul thought about it and then nodded. "I'll be here if you need me."

"You always are." I slapped his arm. "How about that leg up?"

I walked to the edge of the floating hole in the air. The lowest point of the opening was about two feet above my head. I stared up at it then glanced over at Sabrina.

"See you when I get back."

She tried to smile. "You better. You owe me an interview."

Mo'Lock hoisted me up to the opening. I grabbed the edge. It felt hot and spongy-wet, but I was able to get a grip and pulled myself up and over. The next thing I knew, I was in a black expanse and the hole was gone. I was in.

There was nothing but total darkness. I could have been in a stadium or a closet. I couldn't tell. It wasn't the kind of darkness I was used to, but a thick, airless dark without any sign of light or sound. With no plan to speak of, I began to walk into the darkness but no matter how long I walked I couldn't tell if I was making progress. As far as I knew I was walking in place. There was no horizon, no way to judge where I'd been or where I was going.

I stopped, feeling the futility of just walking, and decided to try something. I took out a cigarette and lit a match. The fire swelled up and for an instant I saw something very strange... the barest glimpse of stone walls and smoke. As I stood there smoking, I began to hear a sound nearby. It was a voice laughing.

"Billy?"

There was no reply, but the laughter got closer and began to move around me in a slow circle.

"I know it's you, Billy," I called out. "I know you're there."

The laughter stopped and I squinted as a figure appeared just ahead of me. It was the kid. He walked out of the darkness and stopped within a few yards of me.

"You can't beat me in here, mister," he said.

"Oh yeah? Why's that?"

"I've got friends in here."

"You had friends back home, too," I said, "but you killed them."

There was a very long pause.

"They got scared. Brian said he wanted out."

"Out of what, Billy?"

Billy stepped closer and I could see now that he had changed. His skin was rougher. Instead of acne, his arms and face had sprouted dozens of tiny gray horns.

"The pact. We made a deal and Brian wanted out. You can't just break a deal"

I took a hit off my smoke, keeping it nice and casual. "Yeah, I can see that. What was the deal?"

Billy laughed. "Simple, a little blood for some power."

"So you got the power and all you could think to do with it was hurt people."

That pissed him off. He stepped a little closer, and for the first time I could see that we weren't alone. There were shapes moving in the background, hundreds of them.

"None of this would have happened if your old friend hadn't come snooping around!" Billy spat.

"Maybe, maybe not."

I used my last cigarette to light another. I offered one to the kid. He shook his head.

"So now what, Billy?" I gestured around to the crowd closing in on me. "You and your friends going to kill me too? Then who, your Mom?"

Billy looked genuinely stunned. "No! Why would I kill my mom?!"

"Well, those things—your buddies—are out there causing a lot of trouble. I had to shoot one to stop him from dragging a woman out of her car. What'd you think he was going to do to her? Kill her, rape her, eat her? Could have just as easily been your mom on the way to work."

Billy twitched.

I'd planted that seed of doubt.

In the background, the shapes shifted restlessly. They seemed nervous. A large figure pushed through, coming up behind the kid. I took a step back. The shape was huge and muscular. It was a living shadow, a wall of blackness standing behind the boy who had sold his soul.

"This the deal maker?" I asked.

Billy nodded slowly. His skin looked as if it was clearing. The shape didn't make a sound.

"How'd you get in touch with the big guy?" I asked, trying to keep the conversation nice and easy.

Billy swallowed nervously. "Got it from a book of incantations."

"Sure you weren't listening to the rock-n-roll records backwards? Smoking the moon cabbage?" I winked.

Billy cracked a smile.

"By the way," I went on, "I took a hit off your stash after you took off. Hope that's cool with you."

That got me a full grin. There ain't a teen on the planet that can resist the pot smoking adult. In his rebellious, confused brain, that made me the coolest thing since, well, the last dope smoker he met. It was just that way at that age. Luckily for most, it passes—unless you're me.

His horns looked like pimples again. I had him. I knew the deal: I'd dug around witchcraft as a kid, too. I'd played with the *Ouija Board* and levitated my pals on the tips of my fingers. All kids do it, but this kid went too far because he was tempted. Because some evil fuck gave him a taste of true power.

Suddenly the huge dark shape put its giant, shadowy hand on Billy's shoulder and spoke. "This one is mine."

I flicked my butt and lit another. "That doesn't work for me."

"Then you will die in here."

I feigned fright and took a long drag. "Tell you what, let the pimple factory go. I'll stay here and fight you. You win, you get me and can pretty much do whatever you want after that. Do we have a deal?"

The dark shape laughed.

"I asked you if we had a deal," I added, padding the plan. "I know you're a man who follows deals to the letter. You're bound to them, aren't you? You and me, in front of all your buddies, in *plain sight*. To the death."

The shape laughed again and shoved Billy at me. The kid slammed hard against my body and looked up at me. He looked scared. I didn't blame him. So was I.

"You stay here," I told the kid, "If the hole opens, jump through it."

Billy nodded, near tears. "Okay."

"But you're still in big fucking trouble."

"I know."

Billy stepped away as I looked up at the huge shape. He was about eight feet wide and just as tall, with arms the size of tree trunks and legs to match. He was all shadow, without features, but even through the darkness I could see the familiar horns and cloven feet. The shape was allowing me to see this. It was part of the illusion, but I didn't give a shit. He was just another whining spirit to me, and I knew his weak spot.

The shape roared and came at me. I ducked sideways and transformed faster than I had before. This time it was for real. I went full-blown werewolf as my clothes shredded from my body. As the shape lunged I rolled and kneed him in the gut, sending him to the floor. The crowd gasped in unison.

The shape wasn't down for long, though. He stood right up and smashed down on my head. If I'd been a cartoon, he would have turned me into an accordion. But, being flesh and blood, he broke bones and drew blood. I rolled with the slam and tried to rake his belly. My claws passed through air. Either he was fast or my plan was on course.

Before the next blow could be thrown, I raised my hands. "Wait, wait, wait!"

The shape stopped.

"You're cheating. We had a deal. You are bound by your deals."

The shape loomed silent. The crowd muttered. I glanced at Billy to see if he was okay and he gave me a nod. That's kids for you; one minute they're trying to kill you, the next minute they're your pal.

"What do you mean?" The shape bellowed.

"You're cheating."

The shape looked stunned. "I am not."

Then he let loose with the hard stuff. I knew he would. I just had no idea how much it would hurt.

He waved his hand without touching me. My flesh exploded, ripping beneath my furry pelt. Suddenly I was covered in blood, staggering in unbelievable pain. I fell to my knees. The shadow was shredding the skin from my body.

I looked up at the shape for a split second and saw a milky film between us. It was there! It was the lie. He'd broken the deal and the illusion flickered.

Then he waved his other hand. I heard, then felt, bones snapping inside my body. I cried out. I couldn't help it. The pain was unreal.

"I knew this would be easy," he said, "but not *this* easy. It's hard to believe you're the one I feared would ruin my plans." His voice was thick and cocky, but like all of these assholes, he just had to talk. "It was my idea to show the boy how to use the circles. It was me who trapped you and sent your life spiraling into hell!"

I rolled in my own blood. "It wasn't that big a change, really."

He waved his hand and my fur tore open across my belly. I was hurting and bleeding out fast. If I was going to make this work, I had to do it fast.

I screamed up at him. "You broke the deal!"

He stopped.

He knew I was right. He knew he had a secret.

I pulled myself to my feet and used every ounce of strength to concentrate on my werewolf power. I felt my wounds stop bleeding. I felt the wounds seal shut. As long as I was a lycanthrope, I could regenerate—at least until I lost too much blood.

But the shape saw what I was doing and motioned at me. I felt my blood run cold. He was taking away the virus that made me werewolf. He was curing me of the curse and killing me at the same time. Once human I would die easily, and he knew it.

I stood there wearing nothing but blood and my gun, pointing. "You are bound by the deal! The deal was YOU and me! YOU and me!"

The shape lowered its arm quickly as if some other force pushed it down. Then after a long silence the shape said, "This *is* me."

I grinned and shook my head. "No it isn't. Show your true self. That's the fucking deal. I said plain sight. That means showing your true self, you bastard!"

There was a stunned silence as everybody froze in the shadows. There are few things that bind devils and demons, but one is the sanctity of the deal. I got this one on a technicality.

The huge shadowy form was an illusion for human eyes. I knew it. He knew it, and now everybody knew it. I set him up when I made him agree to fight me in plain sight. I used my wolf form, sure, but I never denied my power. Plus, he felt it inside me. The shadow, on the other hand, lied by omission. Slowly, the illusion faded and I saw the true Deal Maker on the floor in front of me.

I stared down at the master of darkness, revealed. No more than a foot tall, he looked like an overcooked rump roast with little black sticks for limbs, tiny, red eyes, and slits for his mouth and nose. Even though I was in pain, I started laughing.

The little thing on the ground waved its tiny stick arms at me. "So now you know. Still, I will prevail! I have always lived! And I always will! What can you do to me that hasn't already been tried? You win this time, but I'll be back and…"

The little thing on the floor went on and on. Billy was in shock at the demon he had served. I gave the kid a nod.

"You do it," I said. "I'm too fucked up."

Billy stepped forward and raised his foot high. He brought it down on the rump roast demon and splattered him all over the void. I scanned the darkness. All of the winged shapes had receded back into their demonic realm. Today's invasion of the living world was officially a failure.

I patted Billy's back as he helped me limp to the opening. "In case I didn't mention it," I said, "you're still in a shit-load of trouble."

"I know."

"I mean, you can't just go around killing people."

"Yeah," the kid said, "but I bet you've killed tons of dudes."

He had a point, but I wasn't buying it. "Don't even."

Through the rip I could see the trees of Griffith Park and the shimmering view of the city below through the crack. Billy stopped at the opening and looked up at me.

"Man, what am I gonna do? They're gonna fry me."

"Just tell them the truth. Tell them the devil made you do it."

2 5

I'd like to tell you there was a

grand reunion outside the rip, but if there was I'm not the one to ask. I fell out of the hole and hit the grass naked and unconscious. Mo'Lock told me later the only word I said was "Ow".

I woke up in a hospital bed three days later with twenty-three broken bones, four hundred and seventeen stitches, and more bruises, contusions, twists, and pulls then any doctor could count. Both legs and one arm were in a cast, as was my pelvis. They had me in one of those steel halos with the screws. On the upside, I had a morphine dispenser that I drained daily.

Because of the strange nature of the crimes and no solid evidence linking him to any deaths,

Billy Fuller was sent to an institution for mental observation until a trial could be held. Evidently the kid was following my advice; he'd told them the truth.

Of course, they thought the kid was fucking nuts.

Good for him. I hoped he took advantage of his second chance. If he didn't, I'd kill him. I sent him a little note saying so.

When I woke the first time, Sam and Mo'Lock were there waiting for me. Sam was picking a scab next to the nub on the left side of his head he called an ear. Mo'Lock was sitting watching me. If it had been anybody but a ghoul, it would have been sweet. Instead, it freaked me out.

"How are you feeling, Cal?" he said the nanosecond my eyes opened.

"I've been better." I reached for the IV and gave the button a push. "Better now."

I felt fine.

"Look at you laying there, you big pussy!" Sam walked to the side of the bed. "I got hurt too, ya know. You don't see me lying in bed!"

I laughed. Mo'Lock didn't get that he was joking and glared at the old man.

"How'd everything work out?"

"Like nuthin' ever happened. The cops cleaned up all the bodies and intercepted most of the reports. A few stories snuck under the radar. The networks reported that an unexpected eclipse occurred and a gang of toughs attacked some folks. Once again we're in the clear because people would rather keep their head in the sand."

"What about ...," Mo'Lock struggled to find the words, "...the werewolf?"

"Gone. Whatever that freak did to me in there, he stripped me of the power."

Everybody got quiet then, and it had nothing to do with me. It was about what I'd fought. Nobody wanted to face what and who it may have been. It was Sam who finally broached the topic with his usual grace.

"So you think it was the devil-man himself that whupped you?"

I shook my head. "Doubt it. I'd like to think the big guy wouldn't be that easy to beat. If it was, then I'm the luckiest fucker walking the Earth."

Everybody agreed, but all the talk was getting on my nerves. I turned up the IV flow.

Sam had one more thing to ask as I slipped into a drugged-out haze. "Look," he said nervously, "I'm thinking I might move around a bit. You know, get away, see the world and all that crap. I was wondering if you were planning on sticking around LA for awhile and..."

"Yes," I said, "I'm staying. Thith placccccce is..."

And that was the end of that.

●   ●   ●

The second time I came to was better. It was the following day, and I woke to a hand caressing my face. When I opened my eyes, Sabrina was sitting on the edge of my hospital bed. She had a smile on her face and a look in her eyes as she watched me I'd never seen in my life.

"Hey."

"I was wondering if we could do that interview now." She smiled and ran the back of her hand against my cheek.

I nodded. "Sure."

She wriggled on the bed and took her pad and paper, pretending she was about to take notes. "First question: is your name Cal McDonald?"

"Yes."

"Second question: are there really monsters?"

"Look at me."

She pretended to make a checkmark on her pad.

"Okay, and the last question: do you like Sabrina as much as she thinks she might like you?"

"Yes."

She threw the pad aside and leaned close. "Sam Burnett said you were going to stick around awhile. I think that's pretty good news."

"You're just saying that because I have screws in my head."

She kissed me. "I think we could make a good team, don't you?"

"You'll have to check with Mo'Lock on that one. He can be a tad possessive."

Sabrina reached into her bag and pulled out the latest issue off *Speculator*, hot off the press. On the cover was a grainy photo of Mo'Lock and the headline "Confessions of the Undead."

I laughed so hard it hurt everywhere. Sabrina leaned over and pushed my medicine release button. She was the woman of my dreams.

I looked her in the eyes as the haze began to come over me again. "I believe I can hang with you," I said.

She reached out and touched her fingers to my mouth as I faded. I fell asleep with a smile on my face. For the first time in years, I didn't dream about monsters.

· END ·

ACKNOWLEDGEMENTS

Special thanks to
the following:

Ted Adams, John Lawrence,
Ashley Wood, Brian Holguin,
Beau Smith, Robbie Robbins,
Kris (the slasher!) Oprisko,
Alex Garner, Cindy Chapman,
Clive Barker, Mark, Dante
and Geoff, Ann Chervinsky,
Korey Doll, Ben Templesmith,
Gretchen Bruggeman Rush,
Jon Levin, Sam Raimi,
Rob Tapert, Michael Kirk,
Brian Holguin Del and Sue
at Dark Delicacies and my
entire family.

Without their help, support,
and friendship this book
would have not been possible.

-Steve Niles

BIOGRAPHIES

STEVE NILES is the current writer of the monthly comic book HELLSPAWN and Image Comics series FUSED! He has also contributed to several issues of SPAWN, SAM & TWITCH, and is co-writer with Todd McFarlane on the upcoming SPAWN 2 movie. His first comic for IDW Publishing, 30 DAYS OF NIGHT, has become one of the hottest titles in recent memory, and will be made into a major motion picture with a screenplay by Steve himself. Steve began his career by founding his own publishing company, Arcane Comix, where he published, edited and adapted comics and anthologies for Eclipse Comics. His adaptations include works by Clive Barker, Richard Matheson and Harlan Ellison. He has also written for Dark Horse Comics, contributing to titles such as DARK HORSE PRESENTS and 9-11: ARTISTS RESPOND.

Originally from Washington DC, Steve now resides in Los Angeles with his wife Nikki and their two black cats.

ASHLEY WOOD was born in Australia in 1971. An award-winning artist and commercial illustrator, his art is published worldwide on a monthly basis and he has participated in both joint and solo fine art exhibitions.

A Spectrum Award winner, he has also worked on numerous television and movie projects.

His work can be seen quarterly in the pages of IDW Publishing's POPBOT, as well as in the upcoming C.S.I. Comic. IDW is also the publisher of Wood's art books UNO FANTA: THE ART OF ASHLEY WOOD and DOS FANTAS: MORE ART OF ASHLEY WOOD.